I0652936

THE
SPOOK

Tim Frayser

YARD DOG PRESS

The Spook
Tim Frayser
First Edition Copyright © Tim Frayser, 2023

Published by Yard Dog Press at Kindle

Print Version ISBN 978-1-945941-37-5
The Spook
First Edition Copyright © Tim Frayser, 2023

Yard Dog Press
710 W. Redbud Lane
Alma, AR 72921-7247

http://www.yarddogpress.com

Edited by Selina Rosen
Copy & Technical Editor Lynn Rosen
Cover art by Steven Parks

First Print Edition July 1st, 2023
Printed in the United States of America
0 9 8 7 6 5 4 3 2 1

DEDICATION

To my family and friends:
Thanks for putting up with me

Table of Contents

CHAPTER 1—SUNDAY MORNING

The desert sun beat down on the hard, rocky ground. Johnson stepped lightly over the rocks, mindful to not slip on some loose gravel. The guide knew the path much better than he did. Golf ball-sized stones littered the path. He followed the guide up a short slope. As he rounded a boulder, a line of caves came into view. Poked into the mountainside beneath a stony overhang, they looked well-hidden from aerial reconnaissance. He smelled meat cooking.

The guide led him up to the entrance of the closest cave. A man in worn, mismatched fatigues appeared from the shadows, an AK-47 hanging from his shoulder. He exchanged some words with the guide, then pointed to the farthest cave. As Johnson's eyes adjusted to the diminished light of the overhang, he saw many hard men with weapons inside the cave mouth.

The guide led Johnson to the cave at the end. A ledge no more than three feet wide separated the entrance of the cave from a dizzying precipice. This was the most secure point on the site, Johnson concluded. The place they would keep their most valuable treasures. The last stand.

Inside, the guide invited him to take off his hat. The cave was surprisingly roomy. Carpets lined the floor. Three men stood inside the cave, their backs to Johnson. As he entered, they turned, suspicious eyes examining him closely. Satisfied, they stepped aside, moving to the rear of the cave, revealing a man seated on the floor. He looked to be in his sixties, with a long, white beard, clad in a blue turban and comfortable robes of tan and green. It was Gulzar Lajani, wealthy son of a Persian oil billionaire and leader of this ruthless sect of fanatics. The old man's eyes were dark but friendly as he looked up.

"Mr. Johnson," he said, his English tinted with a French accent. "Please, sit down. Sit down. May I offer you some refreshment?" Before Johnson could answer, one of the men in fatigues was already bringing him a cup of tea.

"Thank you, sir," Johnson said, bowing as he accepted the

THE SPOOK

tea. Johnson, who was in his mid-thirties, clean-shaven, with a pronounced chin and small, sharp eyes, wondered how they might be sizing him up. He sat down on the carpet and crossed his legs in the manner of his host.

"We are most pleased with the last shipment of weapons," the old man said. "They have served us well. It has been a productive summer."

"I am most pleased to hear that," Johnson replied. "I have heard news reports of progress against your enemies."

The old man closed his eyes. "Oh, and our enemies are everywhere!" He opened his eyes and looked directly at Johnson. "Please understand," he said, "although many of my people see you as an infidel, I know the truth—please know you are considered a good friend and ally to our cause."

"And I appreciate your friendship," Johnson said, sipping his tea. He sat in the coolness of the cave, knowing full well the old man across from him would shoot him in the head the moment his usefulness came to an end. As was the way of the world. "How does your struggle progress?" A fly buzzed around his head.

The old man sighed. "We have suffered some setbacks. Several of my lieutenants, including my own son, have been arrested in the past month. Our enemies have dishonored us. Reprisals must be made. Honor must be restored. We have a list of required items..." The old man motioned gracefully with his hand, and the man who brought Johnson his tea handed him a small piece of paper.

Johnson read the list. He nodded his head. "I can get you everything here within the week. Will payment be made the usual way?" The fly circled his head and flew up towards the roof of the cave.

The old man blinked slowly. "A deposit will be made to your Swiss bank account, as usual." A young man in fatigues brought him a cup of tea. "And when we prevail, we will not forget our friends. Our cause is just. To victory!" He raised his cup in a toast. The others in the cave shouted their support.

Johnson took a short sip. "If I may ask," he said, "what exactly do you consider victory to be?"

"Why, the destruction of our enemies, or course," the old

man replied.

Johnson looked at the list again. Grenades, small arms, sniper rifles, explosives and ammunition. "This will do it," Johnson admitted. "You will kill many of your enemy with this."

"Of course," the old man said. "Killing our enemy leads to victory."

The fly buzzed in front of Johnson's face again. Lightning-fast, his hand reached out and snatched the fly in midair. He squeezed his hand into a tight fist, and then opened up his fingers. The dead fly lay in the middle of his palm.

"I just killed this fly," Johnson said, turning his hand so that the fly's carcass fell to the carpet. "That does not mean I have achieved victory over the flies."

The old man frowned. "Of course not," he said. "There are always more flies. The future always brings more flies."

Johnson looked up. "What if you could change that? What if you had something that could change the future—allow you to eliminate your enemies and shape the world into your vision, the way you have always dreamed?"

The old man stared at Johnson. "Are you talking about some new weapon?"

"Indeed," said Johnson. "Indeed I am. You could kill your enemies, yes, smash their bodies and scatter their brains. You could satisfy yourself with just killing them... But what if I told you there was something that would not just kill your enemies, but destroy them? Erase their futures. Completely and utterly eliminate them—forever?"

The old man leaned forward; his interest piqued. "Such a thing exists?"

"That is not the question," Johnson said, leaning back on his elbows. He had a cheerful grin on his face. "The question is: how much would you be willing to pay for it?"

THE SPOOK

CHAPTER 2–SUNDAY AFTERNOON

Thunder shook the ground as Ben struggled against the wind. Sheets of rain slammed against his body, borne by the gale-force winds. His eyes stung from the assault of the raindrops. A bolt of lightning struck a tree to his left, blinding him and filling the air with the smell of charred wood. The trees had been so beautiful when he first arrived.

He stopped, and rubbed his face. His breath came in gasps. Ben looked down towards the beach. Waves were still rolling in fifteen feet high. He shook his head. Stupid! So stupid! He should have left the island when he had the chance.

The typhoon had formed in the mid-Pacific several days earlier. A particular combination of atmospheric conditions had created a fierce, awful storm. There had been little concern among the staff of the beachside hotel, since it seemed to be headed out into open water. But then the winds changed, and the monster storm had turned north, straight for Fiji.

Ben was a patent lawyer. He and his companions had been in Fiji for a legal conference. The firm had gone on several similar retreats over the years, to the Bahamas, Rio and Hawaii, and Ben had looked forward to this one. It had started out pleasant enough. The island was as beautiful as he had imagined. Palm trees swaying in the ocean breeze, long, private beaches, and incredible hotel meals. It was paradise. Ben looked down the narrow street, now littered with trees and debris, and wished he had never gotten on the plane. Paradise had turned into Hell.

He ran down the street, each footstep splashing through puddles of water. When the weather reports started coming in, there was an almost festive attitude in the hotel. Some guests started planning "typhoon parties." Those plans fell apart when the full strength of the storm hit them.

He'd been in his hotel room, watching the storm roll in. The mountainous clouds and horrible thunder filled him with dread and drove him to hide in the closet, shaking with fear. He heard a loud thumping sound come up the hallway. BAM

THE SPOOK

BAM BAM! Someone was banging on doors, yelling.

"Everybody up!" the voice cried. "We've got to evacuate the hotel! We have to get to higher ground. The bus is leaving in ten minutes! Everybody out!" BAM BAM BAM! The racket faded as it moved down the hallway.

Ben did not know how long he crouched there in his closet before he mustered the nerve to get up. He opened the door to find the hallway empty. Every room he passed was empty. When he got downstairs to the lobby, he found the front doors open, the wind blowing spray across the carpets and walls.

The air was full of sounds: the howling wind, the rain pelting down on everything, the booming thunder. Ben stopped. There was a new sound: a creaking groan coming from the walls of the lobby. Then came a ripping, tearing sound as deep cracks appeared in the walls. Windows shattered. Ben had been watching TV the day the twin towers fell, and he did not want that to happen to him. That was when he took off running, looking for the bus.

Outside, the rain hit him like a fire hose. Ben looked down the street, litter dancing in the wind, palm trees bending to the gale. His clothes were instantly soaked. Water pooled inside his shoes. He gasped in surprise. Where was the bus? There was supposed to be a bus here to take everyone to higher ground. Where the hell was it? He began to shake with fear. Through a gap in the buildings and beyond the beach, he could see the huge grey mass building on the horizon. As bad as it was, he knew the full force of the typhoon was still miles out to sea, headed straight for him.

"Hey!" he heard off to his left. Ben jumped at the sound. It seemed strange for something so normal to come up in the midst of the storm. He turned, and through the downpour a man was striding towards him. The man had on a long sleeve black shirt, which was soaked and stuck to his trim torso. Short, dark hair flattened against his head. And for some reason, the man was wearing gloves—black, fingerless gloves, like something a biker would wear. They just seemed so out of place.

"Hey!" the man repeated, closing the distance. "You need some help?" The water in the street was up to his ankles.

Ben shook his head. "The bus!" he called out against the roar of the storm. He pointed down the empty street. "The bus taking everybody out of here. It was supposed to be here!"

The man glanced over his shoulder. "I think it's a couple streets over!" he replied. The man reached out a gloved hand and hooked Ben's elbow. "Come on, let's find it!"

Ben let himself be dragged along, sloshing through the flooded streets. The man surged ahead when they got to an intersection. Above them, the rain hammered down relentlessly. "There!" the man pointed off to his right. "There it is!" Ben squinted through the rain. A half a block over, a yellow school bus sat parked next to a dimmed light pole. He could see figures moving around it.

The man waved a gloved hand. "Come on!" he ordered. Ben followed the man in black, both bowing their heads against the wind. They made it about ten feet when they saw the tail lights of the bus. The bus was leaving!

"No!" cried Ben, seized with panic. He sprinted ahead and slipped on the wet pavement. He fell to his knees and fell forward on his hands. Ben gasped the air, thick with rain. He felt like he was drowning.

A hand reached under his armpit and pulled him to his feet. "Come on, you can do it!" yelled the man in black. The sound of an engine starting ahead of them spurred Ben forward. His legs were trembling as he hurried forward. A tremendous wave of relief came over Ben as his hand fell on the side of the yellow bus. He felt a hand patting him on the shoulder.

"You're gonna be all right now," said the man in black. Ben looked forward to the bus driver, standing at the door.

"Come on!" yelled the driver. "You're the last. We gotta get out of here!"

Ben wiped the rain out of his face as he turned around. "Thank you—" he said.

But the man was gone.

"Come on!" said the driver, grabbing Ben's arm. He started pulling him into the bus.

"Hold it," said Ben. "Wait! There was a guy right here—where'd he go?"

The two looked up and down the rainy street. It was completely deserted. An empty can rattled past their feet, borne by the wind.

"He was right here!" Ben insisted.

The driver looked at Ben and shook his head. He put a hand on Ben's shoulder. "Come on," he said, in a quieter tone. "Let's get on the bus."

Ben climbed aboard and headed towards the rear of the vehicle. The seats were full of wet, shivering tourists, holding bundles of clothes or other valuables. Behind him, he heard the doors slam shut, the bus grind into gear, and the engine roar. He found an empty seat just as the vehicle lurched forward and rumbled down the street. The window had fogged up, so he ran his fingers across the plexiglass to look outside. The street was still empty.

Ben sat silently as the bus lurched up the hills, his clothes and shoes soaked with water, his eyes staring out the fogged windows, searching in vain for the man in the black shirt. But he was nowhere to be seen.

CHAPTER 3– MONDAY MORNING

The view out the big windows showed a beautiful, perfectly blue sky. Beyond the parking lot, tree branches silently swayed in the breeze. Spring had arrived in Virginia. The sun rose off to her right, sunbeams filtering through the trees and reflecting off the windshields of the cars parked below. The Potomac River was hidden far behind the trees, but she could imagine its deep blue waters, mist rising under the breeze, rolling down to the sea.

Tabitha Van Brunt took a moment to stand in front of the big windows, drinking in the view. She clutched the bundles of file folders to her chest. She took a deep breath and let it back out slowly, clearing her mind of all stresses and thoughts. She opened her eyes. That was enough. That would last her the rest of the day. She needed a moment of peace before her day started.

She turned and headed down the corridor to the security doors. She shifted the stack of folders to one hand to hold up the card key hanging from her lanyard. The sign above the door read Image Analysis. The door beeped approvingly and unlocked for her. It took at least Level Three clearance to get that far into the building. She nodded to the security guard inside the door as she passed the lounge area. There was something sweet in the air. Somebody brought donuts.

At her cubicle, Tabitha had to move a stack of folders to make room for the latest stack of folders. First email, she decided, then coffee. She had just sat down and logged into the network when a face popped up over her cubicle wall. It was a ruddy face, with piercing blue eyes and topped with thick salt-and-pepper hair.

"Morning, Tabitha." It was Adam Weaver, the section head, her supervisor. Tabitha could smell the coffee he was holding on the other side of the cube wall.

"Good morning, Sir," she replied. But it was not good. It's never good when the boss shows up before you do.

THE SPOOK

"How's your work load this week?" he asked. Tabitha made an effort to not look at the stacks of folders on her desk. She thought of the Vietnamese project, the ongoing Colombian connection, the overdue Balkan report... then realized it was a rhetorical question.

"Not bad," she lied. "What's up?"

"Got an agent from Interpol coming in this morning," Mr. Weaver said. "Level One briefings. But he said he's also got some Level Three stuff I'd like you to look at."

Great, she thought. *Yet another report.* She forced a smile. "Sure thing," she said.

"The meeting's at ten," Weaver said as he turned to leave. "Be ready about noon."

Noon, she thought. *There goes lunch.* Tabitha looked at her computer screen and made a decision. Coffee first, then email.

Three cups of coffee later, Tabitha had finished the synopsis for the Vietnamese project. There had been reports of terrorist activity in the Annam Highlands of the central region, Gulzar Lajani's territory, but the satellite photos were clear and showed no obvious threats. If anything, they showed the deterioration of some rural roadways due to lack of use. She was making some notes when she realized it was eleven forty-five. She saved her report to the server, put her workstation in standby, and grabbed a notepad as she got up. From the hallway, she could see the door to the conference room was still closed. The Level One meeting was still going on. Level One security clearance was only for the higher-ups in the Agency.

Her stomach gave a quiet rumble. Tabitha wondered if she had time to go get a bag of chips from the lounge. That'll teach me to skip the donuts in the morning, she told herself. She started to go back when the door suddenly opened. She folded back behind a pillar. Three older men in expensive suits, all with Level One clearance, filed out of the room and headed down the hallway away from Tabitha. Another man appeared with Mr. Weaver. They shook hands, then the other man left. Weaver looked down the hallway, spotted Tabitha, and waved her to come forward.

Weaver stood at the door and motioned her to go inside. The windowless conference room was empty save for one man sitting on the opposite side of the long table. "Tabitha, this is Paul LeBlanc from Interpol," Weaver said. "This is Tabitha Van Brunt from photo analysis, one of our best." LeBlanc rose to shake her hand. He was shorter than her, with a triangular face and thinning dark hair. Firm handshake, though, she thought.

"Mr. LeBlanc," Tabitha said as they sat down. Weaver sat off to one side while Tabitha sat across from the agent. "What can we do for you?"

LeBlanc produced a briefcase from beneath the table. "Our office in Belgium regularly monitors news broadcasts from all over the world," LeBlanc said, opening the case. He spoke with a vaguely German accent. "Much like your National Security Agency. We recently noticed some instances that may or may not be of some concern."

The Interpol agent pulled a slim manila folder out of the briefcase and closed the latch.

"What kind of incidences?" Tabitha asked.

LeBlanc actually shrugged. "It could be nothing," he said. "A new fashion trend. Fans of some old television show." He opened the folder. Inside were a short stack of 8x10 photographs, color and black & white. He spread them out in a line on the table.

The photos were a mix of interiors and exteriors. Each one focused on groups of people, small and large. Tabitha shook her head. "What am I looking at here?"

LeBlanc pulled a red felt tip marker from a shirt pocket. In the first picture, he circled the image of what looked like a man in a black jacket. He did the same to the second picture—another man in another black jacket. Tabitha frowned. LeBlanc went to each photo in the line, each time finding a man in a black jacket... and what appeared to be black gloves. Tabitha looked up.

"Who are these people?" Tabitha asked.

"That is what we would like to know," LeBlanc replied. "Again, it could be nothing. A coincidence. A simple case of people with some similar style of dress jumping in to help strangers."

"Help strangers?" Tabitha repeated. "What do you mean?"

"What I mean," LeBlanc said, "is that each of these photos was taken within the past sixteen months. Each photo is at the scene of what one might call a disaster, or some drastic event." He went through the photographs. "This photo was taken just after the earthquake in Spain last year. This one was shot near the site of the big train derailment in Tokyo two months ago. And this one," he said, pointing, "was taken by a British tourist during a Free Tibet protest rally in Hong Kong."

Tabitha picked up the picture to look at it more closely. The scene was a narrow street, swirling with chaos. In one corner, the photo showed a man in a black jacket and black gloves helping a bleeding protester out of the line of fire. The photo was annoyingly blurry.

Tabitha put the photo down. "There must be a zillion black jackets in the world. Why is Interpol interested?"

"Interpol is interested in anything that might signal the beginnings of a new political faction," LeBlanc explained. He pointed to the Hong Kong photo. "Especially one that seems increasingly interested in areas of political unrest. Terrorist groups frequently recruit new members from politically disaffected individuals."

Tabitha's eyes scanned the pictures. "These are from all over the world, crossing all sorts of political boundaries. What group would have the resources or the desire to recruit people across the world from each other? It doesn't make sense."

"Good point." LeBlanc scooped up the photos and replaced them in the folder. "If that is what you and your fellow CIA experts determine, Interpol will be satisfied." He slid the folder across the table to Tabitha.

Tabitha looked at Weaver, who leaned forward. "As a gesture of interagency cooperation," Weaver said, "we will be happy to take a look at the data."

LeBlanc rose to leave, the meeting obviously over. "It has been a pleasure to meet you." They stood and shook hands. Weaver walked out with LeBlanc, leaving Tabitha alone in the meeting room. She sighed. She scooped up the folder and left the room.

Halfway back to her cubicle, she met up with Weaver in the hallway. "Sir," she asked, "if Interpol thinks this is somehow related to terrorism, shouldn't Homeland Security be looking at this?"

Weaver shook his head. "Keeping an eye on the world is our job. If it comes to that, we'll pass the info along, but for now we've got the ball. Besides," he added, "Homeland doesn't have the resources we do."

"Resources? What resources?"

Weaver smiled and patted her on the arm. "You," Weaver said cheerfully. He went back to his office.

Tabitha rolled her eyes and walked away.

THE SPOOK

CHAPTER 4–MONDAY EVENING

The laughter of children echoed down the long, tall hallways. Valentin Bravo's eyes were drawn up the ceiling, where a shiny balloon hovered high in the corner, a pink ribbon dangling underneath. He smiled, remembering how magical balloons had seemed long ago, when he was his daughter's age. He stepped out onto the balcony and looked down. The huge living room spread out before him, filled to the brim with squealing children. Colorful streamers crisscrossed the room. A man in a clown costume was juggling rubber balls. In the corner, a table was piled high with brightly-wrapped presents.

Bravo was a short man, with thick, dark hair and a thin moustache. He wore a simple white suit, his shirt open at the collar, and walked like a man satisfied with his position in life. He searched the mass of life below, and found the object of his love: his beautiful daughter Maria, six years old that day, laughing and dancing. It filled his heart with joy to see her so happy.

"Senor Bravo?" said a smiling man to his right. "May I get you something?"

Bravo shook his head. "Everything I want is right here." He stood on the balcony, enjoying the scene below, until he realized the smiling man had not left. "What is it, Juan?"

"It is Senor Johnson, sir," Juan replied. "He asks if he could speak to you at your convenience. In the garden."

Bravo sighed. He pointed to the scene below. "Have the photographer take lots of pictures," he instructed. "I will be back before the cake is cut."

Bravo marched through the rooms of his mansion, past gorgeous antiques, and expensive works of art until he came to a tall pair of glass doors. Through the doors, he stepped out onto a patio overlooking a manicured garden. Roses, tulips, and irises sprouted between carefully trimmed bushes. A gravel path ran between the bushes. On the far end of the garden stood a man in a dark suit. He stood patiently at the rail overlooking the valley below, hands in his pockets. Bravo walked up behind him.

"What is it, Senor Johnson? Why do you bother me on my daughter's birthday?"

The man called Johnson turned around. "Bad news, I'm afraid," Johnson said. He pulled an envelope from inside his jacket pocket. "It seems our acquaintance in Panama, Mister... Shamoun, is it? Your production manager? I'm afraid he has been cheating you."

Bravo frowned, and opened the envelope. Inside were pages with columns of numbers. "Mr. Shamoun has only been sending you half of the product you paid to have cultivated. He has been selling the rest and pocketing the profits. These are statements of his secret bank account in Geneva."

Bravo looked over the statements, then closed his eyes. "This is very disturbing news," he sighed. "I am very disappointed in Mr. Shamoun." He looked at Johnson. "Steps will need to be taken."

Johnson nodded. "Shall I take care of things for you?"

Bravo shook his head. "No. I need you to talk to the Russians about their shipment—it is late, and we have a schedule to keep. And a message to send to anyone foolish enough to steal from Valentin Bravo. I will send Antonio. He will make sure production resumes and a proper accounting is done. He will ... restructure the organization."

Johnson lowered his head. He knew all would be well. Production always flourished under the eyes of the Hook. "I do have some good news," he said. "Our contacts in China have some very interesting new products for us. I am having a shipment routed here through Holland. We already have a customer."

"Weapons?"

Johnson nodded. "Biological."

"Interesting," said Bravo. "You must stay for dinner. We can discuss the details over some most excellent wine, directly from France."

"I would be honored, sir," said Johnson. "But please, do not let me keep you from your daughter's birthday party. There is a present for her in the front hallway."

Bravo smiled and shook Johnson's hand. "Thank you

for your loyalty, my good friend. It is much appreciated. Juan here will show you to your room." Johnson turned to Juan, who led him up some stairs. Bravo watched him leave. A good man, Senor Johnson, he thought. Useful. Practical. A smart man too, he reminded himself. Perhaps too smart. *The day will come when I must bury you*, Bravo thought, waving to his friend below, *but for now… you are a good man.*

Juan returned several minutes later. "Is there anything else, sir?"

"Get me Senor Lopez on the phone, right now!" Bravo ordered. "I will be in my office."

The servant swallowed. "Right away, sir," Juan replied. He hurried to the nearest phone, and noticed his hands were shaking as he picked up the receiver.

Juan punched numbers into the phone. The line clicked. "Hello?" came the voice of Lopez. The voice still sent chills down Juan's spine.

"Stand by for Senor Bravo," Juan said. He walked into the next room and handed the phone to his employer.

"Antonio?" Senor Bravo said into the phone. He smiled, and nodded to Juan to be left alone. Juan turned to leave the room. "Antonio, we have a problem," he heard Senor Bravo say. "A division of the business will need to be reorganized…"

Juan walked down the hallway, back towards the birthday party. He knew from experience how the rest of the conversation would go. He walked past the antiques and expensive works of art. The laughter of children echoed down the hallways. He resigned himself to his fate. As prisons go, Juan thought, it was not a bad one.

THE SPOOK

CHAPTER 5—MONDAY EVENING

The lead truck screeched to a halt on the desolate road. Hot, dusty air billowed around the vehicle. The driver cranked up the emergency brake and opened his door, squinting against the late afternoon sun. The man pulled down the brim of his Yankees baseball cap to shield his eyes. He wore khaki pants and a short sleeved green shirt. A second vehicle came to a halt behind the truck. A middle-aged woman in a striped shirt leaned out from the driver's window.

"What's the holdup?" she called.

The Yankees fan said nothing, but stepped around behind the truck. Sure enough, the right rear tire was flat. He heard doors creak open around him.

The other driver and two passengers now stood on the dusty road. The Yankees fan cursed to himself, and ran a hand across his frustrated face. It had been a long day. The reporter and his cameraman wanted pictures of the whole valley, not just the clinic and village. They even drove out to do a live broadcast at the ancient boab tree outside of town. It had been featured in *National Geographic* magazine once, and was the most famous thing in the remote region... until the famine.

The two drivers stood next to each other. "What are we gonna do now?" the woman asked. Both looked apprehensively to the west, towards the bright setting sun. "We can't be out here after dark," she added.

"I know!" said the Yankee fan in hushed but tense tones.

"Mark," said Brenda, her eyes wide and anxious. "What are we gonna do?"

Mark pulled off his Yankees cap and ran his fingers through his hair. The two passengers were flushed and exhausted from the African heat. Poor Liam looked like he needed a nap. They would be no help with the tire. He looked at his watch. "Okay," he said, coming to a decision. "Gerry! Liam! Get your equipment out of my truck and load it all into Brenda's. You guys go on to the village. I'll fix the flat and then follow you in."

THE SPOOK

The reporters moved slowly, wearily taking cameras and recording equipment out of the lead truck. Mark opened up the back and pulled out the rusty jack.

Brenda squinted at the sunset. "We can't just leave you out here. It'll be dark soon."

"We don't have a choice," Mark replied. He was grateful for the concern, but sighed and patted her on the shoulder. "It's going to be okay. I'll have this fixed in no time, and then I'll be right behind you."

"Hey," came a voice from up the road. Mark looked up and saw a man walking down the dusty track. He wore a long-sleeved black shirt, rolled up to the elbows. His short hair looked strawberry blonde in the fading sunlight. "You folks need a hand?"

Mark looked back at the stacks of boxes. "Um, yeah," he said. He took a step sideways to look at the empty landscape behind the stranger. "Where the hell did you come from?"

"Up the road," the man said, slowing down his pace as he arrived. He wore blue jeans and black jogging shoes. He pointed to the third truck. "Ah, flat tire. Let me get that jacked up for you."

Mark checked on the reporters' progress. They had everything loaded into Brenda's truck with barely enough room for the three of them. The links on the jack clicked as the truck slowly rose off the dry earth. Lug wrench in hand, the lug nuts came off one by one.

Brenda stopped before climbing into the second truck. "You sure there's no other way?" she asked.

Before Mark could answer, the stranger asked, "Where's the spare?" He pulled off his black shirt to reveal an ash grey t-shirt underneath.

"There in the back!" cried Brenda, pointing to the open rear hatch.

"I'll—I mean, we'll be fine," said Mark. "Go!"

Brenda started up the second truck and drove around the stalled vehicle, quickly disappearing into the gathering twilight. The stranger was lugging the spare out of Mark's truck.

"What's your name?" Mark asked.

"Um, Jim," said the stranger, folding his shirt and

tossing it into the open passenger window. Shadows were getting long. Mark cast an anxious gaze at the setting sun, and looked back to see the flat tire flop to the side of the road. The stranger rolled the spare over and adjusted it on the wheel. That was when Mark noticed the man was wearing black leather fingerless gloves.

The western sky was ablaze with brilliant gold and red colors as the stranger screwed the nuts back into place, tightening them with the lug wrench. "Almost done," he said. He looked up to see Mark staring at him, hands on hips.

"Who wears gloves in Africa? Jim isn't your real name, is it?" he asked. The stranger looked up, his face shaded by the fading sunlight.

"Does it matter?"

"Yeah, it matters," said Mark, his Yankees cap pushed back over his forehead. "It's more than ten miles to the nearest town. We're in the middle of nowhere. You came all the way in, through the wild brush, and your clothes weren't even dusty. Where'd you come from? What do you want? Who are you, anyway?"

The stranger put his weight against the tire iron, twisting the last nut on tight. He lowered the wrench down and sighed. "Just trying to help," he said. With his other hand, he reached under the truck and started jacking down the truck.

"Trying to help?" said Mark. "Nobody's helping us out here. The famine has been going on for a year, and all the relief agencies do is give us the runaround. The government says the people here don't need help. They'd be happier if everyone kicked off and died because then they could lease the land to developers. The Foundation is running low on funds and we might get shut down. We're the only clinic for a hundred miles and we have to scrounge and barter for every little bandage."

The stranger cocked his head down the road. "Weren't those guys reporters? Maybe when word gets out things will start happening."

Mark shook his head. "Fat lotta help they are. People are dying out here, and they're just pointing cameras. Shooting pictures doesn't help..."

Both men froze at the sound of a low growl in the high grass off to the south. The shadows were deep in the thick brush. It was hard to tell just how far away the sound came from. Slowly, the stranger stood up, his eyes focused on the brush. He reached for his folded shirt.

In a breathless voice, Mark said, "We should go." When he saw the stranger's puzzled face, he added, "This is lion country."

Mark rubbed a sweaty hand against his pants leg. He turned slowly and looked off to his right, in the opposite direction of the growl. They sometimes hunt in pairs, he remembered. His heartbeat was racing. Mark forced himself to move his feet towards the driver's side door. The stranger had already arrived at the passenger door and was trying to quietly open it, the tire iron still in his hand. Neither men made any sudden movements.

The stranger's eyes rolled to his left, watching for anything moving in the brush. He quietly pulled the door open and slid inside, pushing his wadded shirt out of the way. Mark opened the driver's door, and put his back against the side of the truck, looking all around as he climbed behind the wheel. A slight breeze blew in through the open windows. Both doors clicked safely shut, and Mark breathed a sigh of relief as he reached for the ignition key.

The lioness slammed against the driver's door like a freight train. Both men inside were jarred as the truck rocked on its wheels. The stranger's head hit the window frame of the truck. The tire iron dropped to his feet. The lioness roared, a resonant cry of frustration and anger. Mark leaned away from the open window just in time to miss most of the huge paw slash across his shoulder. The stranger shook his head to clear his senses. He still held his black shirt in his left hand. He twirled his wrist to wrap the shirt around his hand, then punched at the massive paw still poking through the window. The lioness retreated slightly. With his free hand, the stranger grabbed Mark's shirt and pulled him down away from the window.

The lioness growled again, a terrifying, rattling sound. Rows of angry teeth appeared in the open window. The stranger swatted at the creature's paw again, then twisted the ignition key. The engine roared to life. Just then, the stranger spotted the tire iron he'd dropped onto the floorboards. He scooped it up and tossed the heavy tool out the open window, directly at the lion's face. The creature yelped, more startled than hurt, and backed away from the window. Leaning over Mark's frame, the stranger pulled the transmission lever, putting the vehicle in drive, and kicked a foot at the gas pedal. Weary tire bearings squealed as the truck pulled away from the animal.

The vehicle veered off the roadway and into the brush, bouncing and heaving like a ship at sea. From the passenger side, the stranger managed to get control of the wheel and get it back on the road. Ahead, he could barely make out the track by the last, fading light of the day. The stranger had to reach across Mark, who was prone across the bench seat, moaning softly. Blood seeped from under a wide rip in his shirt.

"Hey!" the stranger yelled at Mark. his eyes darting back and forth from the cab to the road ahead. "You okay? Stay with me, now!"

The tiny village of Mabab was a collection of grass and mud huts, houses not much different than what the Pharaohs might have seen as they were passing through. But it was home to ten families of simple farmers and goat herders... sick farmers.

The reporters recovered as night fell and were passing out medicine and blankets. Brenda had stationed himself on top of her truck, looking out over the surrounding stockade for any sign of their missing leader.

"I got headlights!" she said suddenly. A half mile away, a pair of bright lights came over a short hill. Brenda knew right away something was wrong. The truck was coming too fast, and it swerved back and forth across the width of the dirt road.

The headlights illuminated the humble houses and skidded to a halt just inside the compound. "Hey!" came a voice. "We need some help over here!"

Two locals dropped what they were doing and came running. They found Mark in the passenger side of the truck, crouched over in pain. The door was pulled open, and careful hands lifted him out of the truck. Brenda rushed up just as the stranger climbed out from behind the wheel. "What happened?" she demanded.

"It was a lion," the stranger said, a smear of blood across his face, his eyes looking dazed in the glare of the headlights. "She attacked just as we were leaving. We managed to get away, but he's hurt." Two of the volunteers helped Mark

23

around to the front of the truck. The stranger's black shirt was wrapped around Mark's left shoulder. Mark's face grimaced in pain.

Laying him down on the ground, Brenda carefully unfolded the shirt. It revealed two deep gashes across his shoulder. The stranger looked down on Mark with concern. "I tried to stop the bleeding."

"I don't think it's too bad," Brenda said. She looked up at the others. "Let's get him inside."

One of the farmers gasped as he stepped back from the truck. "It really was a lion." Brenda followed his gaze. There were paw prints the size of dinner plates in the dust of the driver's side door. The prints were smeared across the logo of the sponsoring medical foundation.

"Oh, my gosh," she breathed. She looked back at the wounded Mark. "Let's get him inside the hut!" Mark's face was pale, but he was alert and able to walk inside one of the huts, leaning on his friends' shoulders. The stranger followed close behind them.

Inside, Mark sat on one of the hut's few chairs. Someone got him a cup of water. Brenda carefully pulled the black cloth off Mark's shoulder. The slashes had already started to crust over. She opened a bottle of disinfectant and pulled a cotton ball from a little box. A hand appeared and quietly took the black shirt away.

Brenda allowed herself a sigh of relief. And, she chided herself, maybe it was time to thank the stranger and show a little overdue hospitality. Outside the hut, campfires lit up the little village. Stars twinkled above. Brenda's eyes searched in all directions. The stranger was nowhere to be seen.

She went back inside the main hut. Mark was cleaned-up and feeling much better. Brenda gave him a shot of antibiotics and walked him to an army surplus cot. Mark reclined back on the blankets. He looked up at Brenda and gave her a silent thumbs up. He was going to be okay.

She nodded and went back outside. Brenda wandered around the huts, and looked inside a couple, but the stranger was gone. Beyond the campfires of the village, the landscape was pitch black. Did he go back into the brush, she wondered? Where did he go?

CHAPTER 6 —MONDAY EVENING

"**Tell me more about this**—biological weapon you found," Bravo said, pouring another glass of wine for himself.

"As you know, China has had a one-child policy for decades," Johnson said, sitting back in the luxurious armchair. His Cuban cigar was perfect. "As such, the government has been on the forefront of finding new, better methods of contraception."

"So what did you find?" Bravo asked with a laugh. "A killer condom?"

"Something much better," Johnson said with a smile. "One might even say... world-changing."

Bravo looked intrigued. He knew Johnson was not one for small talk. "And how might we profit from such a world-changing drug?"

Johnson knew Bravo well enough to know when he said "we" he meant "me."

"Profit comes from investment," Johnson said. "Our contacts in China can get this specific pharmaceutical to us, but only at a fair market price." He pulled a slip of paper from his coat pocket and slid it across the coffee table to his host. Bravo read it with a grunt.

"And why should I pay such an exorbitant amount for a drug I know nothing about?" Bravo asked.

Johnson leaned forward. "Because, my friend," he said quietly, "it will make you the most powerful man on Earth."

Bravo was interested, but still dubious. "Where is this product now?"

"The port of Rotterdam, in the Netherlands, at a secure location," Johnson added.

"How many people know about it?"

"To our couriers, it is merely one more shipment to be delivered. What it does, no one knows but us and the scientists that developed it."

"Do we need those scientists to make more product?" Bravo

asked.

Johnson shook his head. "The process was lengthy, extensive, and as you can see, expensive, but we can duplicate the product."

"Then these scientists represent a loose end, my friend," Bravo said. "If this product is as valuable as you say, we need to protect our investment and eliminate any possibility of competition."

Johnson frowned. "I see your point, but—"

"Whatever it takes, Senor Johnson," Bravo said, sipping his wine.

Johnson started to reply, but merely shrugged his shoulders. "As you wish," he said, taking out his cellphone. With enough finished product in hand, Johnson found himself agreeing with Bravo: the scientists had outlived their usefulness. The connection made; his instructions were brief.

CHAPTER 7–TUESDAY MORNING

Tabitha completely blew off the "black jacket case" until the next day. With all the other reports on her desk waiting for attention, she figured she had more important things to do than chase a wild goose. At best, it seemed like some kind of make-work dreamed up by the bosses. At worst, it was an unsolvable case that would only look bad on her evaluation. She did not even open the picture folder again until the afternoon, as she sat in her cubicle waiting for a file to download.

Munching on a carrot stick, she idly opened the folder and started flipping through the pictures. There were fifteen in all. Each one had a short paragraph taped to the back explaining where and when they were taken. The pictures could have been random group photos from anywhere in the world... except for the presence of those men in black jackets. All about the same size, all about the same features, but not the same person? She had to admit: that was odd.

With a carrot stick dangling from her mouth, she opened her flatbed scanner and scanned digital images of the photos. There were some printed reports mixed in with the pictures. She set these aside until she was done scanning.

The carrots were still wet from when she washed them that morning. Tabitha absently wiped her hand off on her skirt and called up the scanned images on her computer screen. One by one, she flipped through the pictures. A chime from her computer told her the download was finished. She minimized the pictures and her attention went back to work on the Balkan report.

There had been reports of increased drug smuggling through the western mountains of Kosovo. One report suggested communication with sources in South America. Satellite photos of the Kosovo area showed no significant difference in automobile traffic. Infrared scans of rail traffic were also inconclusive. But that could only mean the drugs were not going by car or rail. Albania was the wild card. Formerly closed to the rest of Europe, it had a population eager to catch up with the rest of the world... and if it had to smuggle drugs to get the cash, so be it.

But something about the Interpol photos kept nagging at her. She minimized the Balkan report and brought up the pictures again. She resized the images and put them into a slide show to compare them. As the images flipped up in succession on her monitor, she skimmed the documents that had come with the photos. They were eye-witness reports from Israel, South Africa, the Philippines, Hong Kong, Mexico... In each case, something terrible had happened: earthquake, flood, forest fire, and in the aftermath of these disasters men with similar dress appeared.

There was more. Other witnesses at the scenes denied ever seeing the men before. They were not neighbors. They did not live nearby. They did not happen to be traveling through the area when the events occurred. In three instances, the men did not appear to even speak the language. And once more, every one of these men somehow seemed to disappear before authorities could question them.

She reread the report from the Israeli Defense Ministry. A man in a black shirt and black gloves broke up a fight in a restaurant in the Arab Quarter of Jerusalem. Before police arrived, however, the man fled the scene. No one in the restaurant had ever seen him before.

Tabitha put the reports down. Fifteen different places over the space of sixteen months— disasters from all over the world. What were the odds random strangers would show up in similar dress? A chill went down her spine. What were the odds the disasters were all that natural?

That, Tabitha realized, must have been Interpol's main concern. There had to be a reason, some sort of logical explanation. Even in cases of random occurrences, there had to be a reason.

Tabitha put aside the Balkan report.

It was after 5 o'clock. On any other day of the week, Tabitha would be on her way home. On any other day, she'd be fighting traffic, cooking supper, checking her email, and curling up with a good book. Today was different.

The office was empty and oddly quiet as Tabitha sat at her desk, staring at her monitor. The slideshow continued to scroll across the screen. There was something there—she knew it. It was almost six, and Tabitha's stomach was growling, so she got up to get a candy bar from the machine. *Snickers or Milky Way?* she thought. *Doritos or Fritos? Decisions, decisions.* She was just about to put her change in the machine when a thought came to mind.

She rushed back to her cube and took the mouse in hand. Two, three images scrolled by, then—there it was. She was looking at a grainy black-and-white picture taken by a security camera in Rome. A Palestinian support rally had turned violent, and people were running through the narrow streets. The camera had been mounted high on a light pole, so it looked down on the crowd. Consequently, it showed few faces. On the left edge of the image was a man in a black jacket, one of the figures LeBlanc had circled in his demonstration. She had looked at the same picture a hundred times that day.

Tabitha zoomed in on the picture. It showed the front of the jacket, only it wasn't a jacket at all. It had two pockets on either side at waist level, like a jacket, but above were two pockets at chest level. At first, she thought it was some kind of hunting jacket, but then she realized what it was. It was not a jacket. Interpol was wrong. "It's a BDU shirt," Tabitha realized. A black Battle Dress Uniform shirt, the same style of army uniform worn by the army from Grenada and the first Gulf War through the "shock and awe" of Kabul.

She scrolled to the next picture and zoomed in close. The picture was dark, and she had to enhance the contrast, but there they were: four big pockets. One by one she checked each picture. A third of them were too grainy, or showed the figure in question from the rear, but by the time she was done inspecting Tabitha was convinced. All the men in the pictures were wearing the same thing: black BDU shirts.

Tabitha felt proud of herself, like she had just solved one piece of a big puzzle. She'd figured out something even Interpol had missed. The final picture was still way off, but for now, she thought, it was a good day's work.

Tabitha put her files away, tidied up her desk, and shut down her programs. She was just about to log off the network when she got an idea. She pulled up the image files she had been browsing through and zipped them into a compressed file. She then emailed the file as an attachment to a fellow analyst upstairs. Her email read: "Please run facial analysis software on specified individuals in these images and reply with result."

There, she thought. If the men in these pictures have any kind of criminal or terrorist background, they could be ID'd—and if the Agency knew who they were, they could figure out what their plan was.

CHAPTER 8— TUESDAY EVENING

Johnson climbed out of the private jet, the cool breeze refreshing as it came off the mountains. There was not much else to see. Besides the airstrip, empty landscape stretched out in all directions, ringed on the horizon by purple, brooding mountains. He noticed that as remote as the location may be, the Chinese kept the grass tidy and manicured. He always admired Chinese efficiency.

The jet had pulled up to an aging hangar at the end of the runway. Dusk was fast approaching, and there were lights in the adjoining facility. A vehicle came around the far corner. It came to a stop several yards from the jet. A man with a familiar face stepped out of the Land Rover, dressed all in white.

"Comrade Johnson!" the man said, extending his hand in greeting. "This is a surprise. We were not expecting you. I trust the product has been delivered to Hamburg with no complications?"

"None whatsoever, Mr. Hong," Johnson said, shaking the man's hand. "I was refueling in Karamay and thought I might stop to congratulate you and your team on a job well done."

"That is too kind of you, Comrade," Hong replied. He looked up, and was astonished to see several men in jumpsuits carrying crates out of the plane.

"If you would please, Mr. Hong," Johnson said, "gather your people in the conference room for a little ceremony."

Hong snapped to attention. "Right away, Comrade!"

Hong summoned the other scientists and ordered everyone to report to the conference room. When he joined his fellow scientists, he found the room had been transformed into a buffet, with seafood, sushi and buckets of champagne. An arm went around his shoulder, and he found Johnson at his side.

"Is this everyone? All the people associated with the project? I wouldn't want to leave anyone out."

Hong did a quick head count of the room. "Everyone is here, yes."

THE SPOOK

"And I trust all the computers have been wiped of important information?"

"Of course, Comrade," Hong said. Johnson had an open champagne bottle in the other hand and took a swig. "Everything is as you instructed."

"Excellent!" He led Hong to the front of the room. All around, the scientists were eating, chatting, and drinking. Johnson unattached himself from Hong and tapped a wine glass.

"Attention, everyone," he said. "Mr. Hong, would you please translate?" Hong nodded, picking up a glass of wine. "Thank you! I am here to announce your work is outstanding, and your efforts are appreciated!" Hong translated, the scientists responding with smiling faces.

"Please, enjoy the wine and food. You have all done excellent work and have made your country proud!" The scientists applauded. In the back of the room, the men in jumpsuits waited patiently. Johnson picked up an empty glass and poured himself a drink, but not from the table. He used the silver flask from his breast pocket.

It only took a matter of minutes. One by one, the scientists got dizzy and sat down in chairs, smiling and chatting happily until their last breath. If Hong suspected anything, it was too late. Johnson watched as he too closed his eyes for the last time. When all was silent, Johnson waved one of the jumpsuited men to come forward.

"Search the facility," he instructed, putting down his glass. "Double check everything. Then spread the accelerants and set the charges. Take the vehicles and dump them. I have a plane to catch."

Johnson had the pilot circle around the facility one last time. The light from the flames lit up the remote landscape of Xinjiang Province. He sat back in his seat, satisfied with a job well done. Logically, he knew missions like that were best left to subordinates, but there was no satisfaction in having others do your work for you. He enjoyed his work.

He poured himself a stiff drink from the galley. He relaxed in his recliner and put on some jazz music. He was a man with no regrets. Some jobs were too important to outsource.

CHAPTER 9—WEDNESDAY

"Hey, Van Brunt," came a voice as she poured herself a steaming cup of coffee. It was Marshall, the data entry tech. "One of the guys upstairs said he had something for you. Sent you an email."

"Oh," said Tabitha. "Okay, thanks." For a moment, she hoped the "guy upstairs" was not Duffy, the database systems analyst. He always smelled like Cheetos. She was back at her desk with her fresh cup of coffee when she remembered the "black shirts." They must have gotten a hit. She logged on to her computer and opened her email. The message from the subject analysis tech made her frown. It read simply, "Facial recognition software estimates 86 percent match."

Eighty-six percent match? Tabitha thought. Match with who? The analysis was useless unless it came up with IDs of at least one of the subjects. She looked up the tech's number in the online personnel directory and called his extension.

"Gannon," came the reply.

"Hank, this is Tabitha Van Brunt," she said.

"'Morning," Gannon said.

"Hank, I don't understand your note," she said, looking at it on her computer screen. "You know, about the pictures I sent you? You said the faces in the pictures were an eighty-six percent match."

"Yeah, that's right." What, she wondered, was he dense or something?

"But, who? Who do they match with?"

"Each other."

Tabitha blinked. "What? What did you say?"

"They're the same person," Gannon said. "The facial analysis software scanned all the faces, and they're all the same person. Some register a closer match to each other than the rest, but on the average there's an eighty-six percent chance they're all the same guy, more than enough for positive confirmation."

THE SPOOK

Tabitha absently called up the image slideshow on her monitor. The faces began to scroll past one by one. It was not a global conspiracy. It was all the work of one man. "But," she said finally, "were you able to identify the subject?"

"No," said Gannon. "Whoever it is, he's not in our criminal or terrorist databases. If we start running the other databases, it might be weeks before we get a hit."

One man, Tabitha thought. One man was on site at each of those disasters. "Do it," she said.

"What?"

"Start running the database scans. We need to know who this guy is."

She could almost hear Gannon shrug his shoulders. "Okie dokie. I'll let you know if we find anything." Gannon hung up. Tabitha sat back in her chair. She watched the images scroll by. Hong Kong. Spain. Tokyo. Rome. It was the same man in all those places. He was on the scene of all those disasters.

Different reasons bounced through Tabitha's brain. He had to be somebody that could travel all over the world—someone who would have business being in different countries. The World Health Organization would have people all over the world... so would the United Nations. Maybe he was a news reporter. That would explain why he appeared at so many disasters... She shook her head. He would have a press tag or some kind of credential around his neck. He would be on TV or in print, reporting on it all. Interpol would know who he was. He would have reported on those disasters. Besides, no reporter could possibly be at all of them.

The pictures on her monitor scrolled by. Tabitha wondered how many more images there were out in the world, how many other places he had shown up. Who was he? Where did he come from? There he was, over and over, usually in the middle of a crowd of people: refugees, victims, emergency personnel, police officers...

Police. Tabitha blinked. If police were on hand, there might be police reports, with eye-witness statements. There could be additional pictures, too: surveillance tapes, maybe mug shots. Tabitha made a list of the cities where the man had appeared, alongside with dates of the events. She then opened up her Internet browser and started searching for police contacts. She typed with determination. There had to be more information out there somewhere.

Two hours later, Tabitha was at her supervisor's office door. "Sir," she said, knocking on the door. "May I have a word with you?"

Weaver looked up from the papers scattered across his desk. "Sure thing," he said. He took off his glasses. "What's on your mind?"

He watched the young woman step into his office, her arms burdened with multiple file folders. "It's that Interpol issue, sir," she explained.

"Don't tell me you found something?" Weaver said. "Come in ... and shut the door."

Tabitha closed the door behind her and hurried to the desk. She set the folders down on the corner. "I think Mr. LeBlanc was correct, sir," she said. "About the pictures of those men. I think there is something very important going on."

Weaver listened. "Such as?"

"For one thing, it's not men—it's a man," she explained. She took a handful of photos out of the original folder. "They're all the same man."

"What?" Weaver said, looking at the photos. "All over the world? That's ... impossible."

"That's what I said," Tabitha admitted. "But the facial recognition programs confirm it: it's the same guy." She cocked her head to look Weaver in the eye. "And I think I know who it is."

Weaver frowned with skepticism. "How could you possibly know that?"

Tabitha picked up another folder and drew out a photocopy. There was an ornate letterhead, with scrollwork circling a crown. "This is from the Hong Kong Police Force," she explained. She moved to the side of Weaver's desk to better point things out. "After this demonstration," she said, picking up the photo of the street protest, "the police collected statements from all the local merchants. They treated the protest like a crime scene: pictures, statements, and they dusted all over the place for fingerprints."

Weaver stared at the mass of data she brought in with her.

"You've been busy, haven't you?"

She pulled out another sheet of paper, with swirling lines and circles. "I had them send me copies of everything they couldn't identify," she said. "Then I did a search to ID the prints. There was nothing in the criminal databases, so I branched out into driver's licenses, state records, and finally military records." She stopped, and waited for Weaver to look up at her.

"I got a hit," she said, "on the database of Iraqi war veterans. The partial print they found in Hong Kong is a 50% match with a man who served in the National Guard. Sir," she said, her voice serious, "I want you to look at this man."

Tabitha slipped out a paper and laid it in front of Weaver. It was the official army record of a Bailey, James Donald, private, Pennsylvania National Guard. The top left quarter of the page was a color photo of a man in dress uniform, showing his head and shoulders. Weaver was looking closely at the photo when Tabitha started laying other pictures next to it. Each photo was an enlargement of the pictures LeBlanc had brought from Interpol. Enlarged to scale and computer-enhanced, they each showed a young man with short curly hair.

Weaver inhaled sharply. "They're all the same," he declared. "It's the same man."

Tabitha nodded. "I know! This guy, Bailey, or whatever his name is, has been all over the world, and every place he's been, something bad has happened. That can't be a coincidence."

Weaver sat back in his chair. "I agree," he said. "Where is this man Bailey now?"

Tabitha consulted her notes. "According to the Bureau of Veteran's Affairs, he's living up north in Pennsylvania— Harrisburg."

Weaver looked over the photos again. "What does this guy do?" he asked. "Is he a salesman? An engineer? What?"

Tabitha arched an eyebrow. "He's a librarian," she said. "According to the IRS, he works at the Eisenhower Public Library in Harrisburg."

Weaver rubbed his chin. "That can't be," he decided. "If this is the same guy, he can't be all across the globe on a librarian's salary. He must be up to something."

Tabitha nodded. "I agree, sir. He must be deep cover for some organization."

Weaver sat back in his chair, overwhelmed by the implications. "What's he up to? Who is he working for? How did he manage to stay under the radar this long? And if somebody like this could be hiding as a simple librarian, how many just like him might be hiding out there?" Weaver drummed his fingers on the desk. Tabitha knew from experience he was thinking hard.

Weaver pressed the button for his secretary. "Get MacKenzie in here," he decided. Brad MacKenzie was the Agency under-secretary of domestic investigations, the liaison with the FBI. "I want him involved in this. This guy," Weaver said, stabbing his finger at Bailey's military record, "could be some kind of ultra sleeper. We're gonna need his bank records, medical records, I wanna know what he had for breakfast!" Weaver looked up. "Good work, Tabitha. Good work indeed!"

Tabitha smiled proudly. She walked back to her desk feeling pretty good about herself. She wished the family members who had laughed at her for joining the CIA could see her now.

Not long after lunch, Tabitha found herself in a company SUV, headed north on the interstate. Tabitha sat with Randall Conrad, MacKenzie's point man, going over records and making plans. Joining them was FBI Agent Steve Baird, coordinating on his smart phone. Tabitha thought Baird looked like a fireplug in a suit: stocky, barrel-chested and no neck. Probably played football in high school, she thought.

"So," said Conrad, sitting back in reclining seat, "what do we know about this Bailey person?"

"The guy is a real Boy Scout," said Baird, scrolling through screens on his phone.

"How so?" asked Conrad. "Is he perfect or something?"

"No," said Baird, "I mean, he really was a Boy Scout. Cub Scout first. Grew up in Delaware until his parents divorced, then moved with his dad to Granite City, Illinois. He made Eagle Scout by the time he was seveteen." Baird pulled out a notebook and flipped through some pages. "The guy donates blood at the Red Cross, volunteers at the local homeless shelter, gives money to charity..."

"Criminal record?"

"None that we can find," Baird said. "He's never even had a traffic ticket."

Conrad opened a can of soda pop from the little cooler. "What about his military service?"

"He was in college when 9-11 happened. As soon as he graduated, he dropped what he was doing and joined the Pennsylvania National Guard. Served one tour in Iraq. Came home and got a job at the library." Baird closed his notebook.

Conrad frowned. "Only one tour in Iraq? Even with all the stop-loss stuff the army's been doing? They've been sending everybody back for two, three tours."

"Nope," said Baird. "He never went back. In fact, nobody in his whole platoon has ever been back."

"That seems odd," said Conrad.

"He helps build houses with Habitat for Humanity," Baird added. "With all that going on, it's kinda hard to believe he even has time to be an international terrorist."

Tabitha frowned. "He fits the profile," she countered. "The photos prove he's been all over the world. The photos are all of him."

Baird shrugged his wide shoulders. "I'm just saying... computer programs have been wrong before. That's all."

"Every time you read about a terrorist," Tabitha said, "the news always talks to his neighbors. And they always say what a loner he was, kept to himself, stuff like that. What if the terrorists recognized that? Suppose they figured the best place to hide somebody was in plain sight, right out in the open?"

"I agree," Conrad said. "A good spy blends seamlessly into his surroundings. He will look just like everyone else. Being a do-gooder might put him right where his bosses need him to be."

Tabitha pointed to the notes Baird held. "Look at his service record. He was in Afghanistan for a year. Maybe he made contact with someone."

"Maybe he did," Baird said. "He helped the engineers with several local projects. He was busy putting in sewer systems, getting electrical power lines strung. His unit helped dig a well for a remote village... The guy does have an impressive skillset. It's possible he was influenced by seditious characters... On the other hand," Baird continued, "It's also possible to get tunnel vision: to start seeing only what you want to see. It's not hard to find a terrorist if you see them everywhere. I'd like a little more proof before we start going after a guy who seems to be a loyal, hard-working American."

Tabitha said nothing. Was Baird right? No, she decided quickly. The proof was there. And when they confronted the man in black with the truth, she was sure, his secrets would all come out.

The SUV made the trip in an hour. Tabitha watched out the window as the car passed signs for Civil War battlefields. They came into Harrisburg and followed city streets to a garage near some railroad tracks.

Tabitha followed Baird and Conrad as they exited the vehicle, voices echoing across the wide spaces. Two Pennsylvania Highway Patrol cruisers and four state troopers standing by. A man in a dark suit came across the concrete floor and shook hands with Baird.

"He's from the state attorney's office," Conrad said, leaning close to Tabitha. "Confirming the federal search warrant on Bailey's house. We've already confirmed he's at work right now." Tabitha noticed a man in a khaki uniform standing off to one side: a county sheriff's deputy.

She felt a sense of pride. "Everyone is joining forces towards a common good," she said quietly.

"Not so much," Conrad said in low tones. She didn't realize he heard her talking to herself. "If this guy turns out to be some kind of super spy, they just all want to be in on the glory of catching him."

Tabitha gave him a sour look. She imagined Conrad being the kind of person who ruined a movie by talking in line about the ending.

Baird and the state attorney looked over the legal papers. When everyone was satisfied, he gave the signal, and everyone piled into the vehicles. It was a short drive across town to the library, down the street from the National Civil War Museum. Clouds on the horizon offered a chance of rain.

Tabitha rode in the back of one patrol car with Conrad. She found the cramped conditions intimidating. Two troopers sat in front. The one on the passenger side spoke to someone on the radio, then turned to face them. "A trooper on the scene says your guy doesn't look like he suspects anything."

The short convoy pulled off the interstate. They drove down narrow streets lined with restored vintage buildings. Joggers in sweat suits and headbands trotted down a sidewalk. At last they came to a stately brick structure across the street from a park. It had a wide set of steps out front and high, clean windows. Young people with backpacks sat outside reading, oblivious to the group exiting the vehicles.

Conrad walked over to speak to the state attorney. "Ms. Van Brunt and I will go in alone," he explained. "Have the state troopers take up position at all the exits. They can cover us in case he tries to make an escape."

Hold it, Tabitha thought. *What?* Before she knew what was happening, Conrad was escorting her up the wide steps, a single state trooper following close behind.

"What are we--?" she began to protest.

"I need you there to make the ID," Conrad explained. "And because nobody knows this guy better than you. I've got your back if there's any trouble." In seconds, they were at the door, Conrad going in first.

Tabitha followed him into the library lobby. She passed the check-out desk and a rack of free literature: local events and places to visit. A little boy was looking at a poster of a frog reading a book. A row of computers sat on a long table. The walls were painted in soothing pastel colors. A young woman and a small child were checking out a couple of books at the counter...

And there he was. Tabitha froze, catching her breath. He was standing behind the counter typing at a computer terminal. He had the same face, same hair, same eyes as the men in the Interpol pictures. Only this man was real. A chill ran down her spine. For Tabitha, it was like spotting a movie star in the supermarket—she did not know how to respond.

He wore a light blue polo shirt. An ID badge was clipped to his lapel. He seemed to find whatever it was he was looking for on the computer, because he made a note on a slip of paper and got up. He took a few steps and then picked up a phone that had been lying on another counter. A nod, a smile, and he hung up, as if he was answering somebody's question. He was acting like a librarian would be acting. Perfectly natural.

A good spy blends seamlessly into his surroundings, she remembered.

Tabitha noticed Conrad standing at her side. He was watching the man as well. The expression on his face was very serious. He was waiting until the man was alone. Conrad looked over to his left and nodded at the uniformed state trooper standing watch near the door. He handed his briefcase to Tabitha. "Stay here," he advised under his breath. Tabitha nodded, and Conrad stepped up to the counter. The state trooper followed close behind. He caught the man's eye as he approached.

"Excuse me," Conrad said, pulling out his credentials, "I'm looking for James Donald Bailey."

"That's me," said the man cheerfully. "What can I do for you?"

"My name is Randall Conrad," he said, leaning forward as he opened his credentials. "I'm with the Central Intelligence Agency. I'd like to ask you a few questions."

The man looked at the ID badge and almost laughed. "Wow, really?" he asked. "Is this a joke?" The man looked at the trooper standing behind Conrad but said nothing.

"No," said the agent. "No, it is not a joke. I assure you this is completely serious. Is there some place where we can talk?"

The man called Bailey shrugged and looked at the big clock on the wall. "Yeah, sure. I got a break coming. Margaret," he said to a woman behind the counter, "I'll be right back, okay?" Bailey stepped out from behind the counter and motioned for the two men to follow him. "There's a quiet room down around the corner." Bailey led the way past rows of children's books. Conrad looked over his shoulder and motioned for Tabitha to follow them. She hurried along, behind the trooper, briefcase in hand.

The group passed a big poster of an elephant reading a book and turned into the empty quiet room. There was a small table with two plastic chairs. It was a tight fit, with the four of them, but Conrad closed the door behind them. "Sit down, Mr. Bailey," he instructed. Bailey sat down in the chair behind the table. Conrad sat facing him, with Tabitha and the trooper flanking the door. Tabitha could not get over how normal the man looked and acted.

"This is Trooper Siegel," said Conrad, "and this is Ms. Van Brunt, one of our analysts."

"Hi," said Bailey. He sat back in the chair. "What's this all about?"

Siegel pulled a folded paper out of his jacket pocket. He handed it across the table to him. "Mr. Bailey," the trooper said, "this is a search warrant for your place of residence. State troopers are searching it now, as we speak."

Bailey frowned as he opened the folded paper. "You're searching my house?" he asked. He seemed more surprised than angry, and a touch amused. "Why?"

"Suspicion of espionage, Mr. Bailey," said Conrad.

Siegel stepped back to the door.

Bailey cocked his head to one side, as if he had not heard correctly. He squinted his eyes at Conrad. "Espionage?" he said. "Are you serious?"

"I assure you the United States government takes espionage very seriously," Conrad said. He looked back at Tabitha, reaching for the briefcase. She handed it forward, and as she did her eyes met with Bailey's. He had brown eyes, the color of coffee. Tabitha stepped back as Conrad set the case on the table and opened it. He pulled out the folder of photographs.

"Mr. Bailey, have you ever been to Hong Kong?" Conrad asked.

"I don't travel much," Bailey said. "Except for Afghanistan. National Guard."

Conrad placed the Hong Kong protest photo on the table. "Then how do you explain this?" he asked.

Bailey leaned forward to look at the picture. The expression on his face was completely blank. "Explain what?"

Conrad pointed to the black-shirted figure. "Do you deny that's you?"

"How could it be?" Bailey replied. He looked close. "You think this is me? When was this taken?"

"February 4th," Tabitha said, speaking up.

Bailey thought quietly for a moment. "The first week of February... we were doing inventory down in non-fiction. I had stuff to do that week. How could I have been in Hong

Kong? That's on the whole other side of the world."

Conrad pulled out another photograph. "This was taken after the train accident outside Tokyo last year," he said. "Look closely at this individual."

Bailey looked close. "Is that supposed to be me, too?"

Conrad was starting to get frustrated. He pulled out the Spanish earthquake photo. "Mr. Bailey, I'm only going to ask you one time: what were you doing in Spain?"

Bailey shook his head. "You think I was in Spain?"

Tabitha could not contain herself any longer. "These are all pictures of you, Mr. Bailey," she said, stepping forward again. "Your image has been confirmed by facial recognition analysis to over an eighty percent probability. These pictures prove you were in a dozen different countries in the past year and a half."

Bailey looked at the pictures spread out across the table. He shrugged his shoulders. "Look, I admit there's some resemblance," he said, "but folks tell me all the time they know somebody that looks like me. One of the grade school kids says I look like some movie star. I kinda have one of those faces. Or so I'm told."

There was a knock at the door. Trooper Siegel opened the door a crack, and they whispered to a second trooper for a few moments. Tabitha looked back at Bailey, who simply sat patiently in his chair.

Siegel closed the door. "Our men just finished going through your house," the trooper said ominously. "We found the shirt, Mr. Bailey," he said. "Your black BDU shirt. It was in with your clean laundry. And the biker gloves." The three stared at Bailey for a reaction.

"Okay," he said calmly. "So?"

Conrad's neck was starting to flush. "What are you doing with a black BDU shirt, Mr. Bailey?"

He shrugged his shoulders. "I like how it feels. I got used to wearing them in the National Guard. They sell them down at the army surplus store downtown. I like all the pockets. I've even worn it here to work a couple of times."

"And the gloves?" Siegel interjected.

"I use them when I ride my bike," he said. "For long-distance runs. I don't understand why you're so concerned—why the government would be so concerned. They're just a pair of gloves. Have I done something wrong?"

THE SPOOK

Tabitha leaned forward again. She pulled out the rest of the photographs and spread them out across the table. "Every man in these photos is wearing a black BDU shirt—and black biker gloves—like what you own!"

Bailey held up his hands. "So? Am I the only person in the world that wears a black shirt once in a while?"

Conrad leaned forward. "What did you do this past weekend, sir?"

"Stuff around the house," Bailey said, shrugging again. "Watched some TV, I guess."

Conrad turned to glare at Tabitha. She gasped as she suddenly remembered. "The fingerprint!"

"That's right!" said Conrad, turning back to face Bailey. "Chinese police found a partial fingerprint at the scene of the Hong Kong protest. It was your fingerprint, Mr. Bailey. It has been confirmed by army records and the FBI. Your fingerprint was found on the other side of the world. How do you explain that?"

Bailey was looking over the photos on the table. He clicked his tongue. "I dunno," he said absently. "How do you explain it?"

Conrad tapped his foot impatiently; he heard the state trooper behind him sigh. Bailey was going through the photos, flipping them over and reading the notes on the backs. "Is this what the CIA does all day?" he asked. "Look at pictures? It's a lot different in the movies."

The interview was not going as Tabitha had imagined, either. They had been unable to pin Bailey down on anything. The presence of law enforcement did not make him nervous. He seemed to have an answer for everything. Conrad turned to face Tabitha and was about to say something when Bailey interrupted him.

"Hey, um, look," Bailey said, "I know you guys are just doing your job and all, think you're barking up the wrong tree here. Also," he added, looking back and forth between the notes, "I think some of your data is inaccurate."

Tabitha blinked. "Inaccurate? What are you talking about?"

"Okay, you guys think these pictures are all of me, right? Well, look," Bailey said. He turned two different pictures around to show the group. "These pictures all have timestamps on them. This one here says it was taken at 4:06 AM on March 3rd in Rome, local time. This one here says it was taken in Manila at 6 AM. Both March 3rd. The same day, two hours apart." Bailey looked up. "Rome and Manila are thousands of miles apart, in different time zones. There's about a five or six hour difference between them."

"What?" Tabitha scooped the papers out of Bailey's hands. "What?"

Bailey looked directly at Conrad. "I think it would take longer than two hours to get from Rome to Manila."

Tabitha noted the times. Her eyes darted back and forth, reading and re-reading the notes. The numbers seemed to frown at her. The times swirled around in her head, clicked together, and fell into place.

The air seemed to drain from her lungs. How could she have missed this? Her shoulders slumped. Bailey was right. Even if he took a military jet, there was no way he could have made it from Rome to Manila in two hours. It was physically impossible. She glanced back at Trooper Siegel, who was rolling his eyes.

"Ms. Van Brunt," grumbled Conrad. "Could I speak with you alone outside?" The trooper was the first out the door. He headed down the hallway towards his colleagues in the library lobby.

Tabitha's mind was spinning. How could she have missed the timestamps on the photos? She realized her hands was shaking. Conrad closed the door behind him. Bailey was still sitting behind the table, surrounded by photos, his face bland and emotionless.

The two were alone in the hallway. Conrad's face was livid. "I do not believe this! Do you realize the resources we had to deploy for this?"

"Look," Tabitha said quickly, "all the data pointed to him. The fingerprint, the recognition software—"

"And a ludicrous presumption that people can defy the laws of physics?" Conrad shot back. "I don't believe this. If this gets out, we could both be fired! Now you get back in there right now and apologize!" Conrad growled. "If he decides to sue the government for harassment, we'll be the laughing stock of the intelligence community! You can finish explaining to me on the way back to Washington!"

Tabitha watched in defeat as Conrad stomped down the hallway. She took a deep breath and opened the door to the quiet room. Bailey was sitting calmly right where they left him.

"Mr. Bailey," she said quietly. "Obviously, a huge mistake has been made. On behalf of the CIA, we apologize for any distress we... for anything I may have caused."

Bailey blinked. "You?"

She sighed. "This is all my fault, sir. I'm the one that went through these security photos and decided you were the subject. You have every right to be angry. If you're mad at anyone, it should be me." She started scooping up the photos and replacing them in the manila folder.

Bailey watched impassively. "You're just doing your job," he offered. "I understand. You guys didn't mess up my house too badly, did you?"

Tabitha closed her eyes in shame. "I hope not, Mr. Bailey. I hope I still have a job when I get back... Again, I am truly sorry." She left the room and closed the door behind her.

The group that had assembled so efficiently for the confrontation disappeared by the time Tabitha got back to the car. Tabitha sat in the back of the car, her hands on the bundle of photos in her lap: the stack of pictures that had been dumped on her and landed her in the middle of this whole mess. Conrad sat across from Tabitha tapping on his smartphone. For the whole trip back to Washington, he did not say a word to her. He concentrated on his phone and making notes in a small pocket calendar. Tabitha did not listen as he made a couple of short calls. She, for her part, was too embarrassed to start any conversations. She flipped through a magazine, skimming the articles but mostly glancing at the pictures. The sun was bright outside the windows.

Conrad broke his silence only when they had arrived at the Langley parking garage. He got out of the car and looked back at her, his expression much more relaxed.

"Okay, I cleared it with the Pennsylvania FBI office and the state troopers," he said. "We're chalking this all up to an inter-agency exercise; intelligence gathering, communications test, that sort of thing."

Tabitha nodded silently. Conrad could see she was upset. He cocked his head to one side. "Everybody screws up once in a while. Don't worry about it."

"Okay," Tabitha said, climbing out of the vehicle. "Thanks."

"But if I were you," he said, walking away, "I'd bring your boss some donuts in the morning." The parking garage echoed with his footsteps. The late afternoon sun slashed rays of light through the shadows. She stood alone.

THE SPOOK

CHAPTER 10– THURSDAY MORNING

After a restless evening, Tabitha eventually fell into a deep sleep that night. She woke the next day running late, and busied herself with the basic routines of her average morning. The day was bright and sunny. The drive to work was easy and clear. She listened to the news on the radio.

"In international news," the reporter said, "Chinese officials are denying internet rumors of a mass murder at a research facility in Xinjiang Province. Officials admit there was a fire at the center but deny any casualties."

Tabitha remembered what Conrad said. She stopped on the way to work to pick up a box of donuts for everyone. The box was warm in her hands as she carried it into the building.

"Morning," she said, nodding to the security guard. Ahead, she could smell fresh coffee brewing in the break room. Tabitha was in a good mood when she turned a corner and almost walked right into Weaver. She had almost completely forgotten about the fiasco in Harrisburg.

"Um, good morning, Sir," she said.

Weaver looked up from a report he was reading and frowned in thought. "The Colombian police are waiting for an update on the Bravo situation. General Cortez is getting anxious."

"I'll have a report on your desk by noon," Tabitha said.

"Make it ten," Weaver said, turning away.

Tabitha did some quick calculations in her head, thinking of all the sources she had to contact. She could make it by ten. But then she noticed Weaver had not left. He turned slowly, and leaned close to her.

"About yesterday," he said, his voice low and reserved. "Forget about it. We'll just count the whole trip as research ... following up on a lead, that's all. The Company is just going to file that away as experience. All right?"

Tabitha nodded. "Yes, sir," she said. "Research."

"This office has a lot more important problems to solve than chasing ghosts for Interpol," Weaver said. "The Pennsylvania

THE SPOOK

Highway Patrol got to sit at the big kid's table this week, so everybody's happy." He turned and left before Tabitha could reply. Her fears were gone. She still had a job. She could forget all about the incident.

Only Tabitha could not forget. Her mind would not let it go. She walked alone down the hallway. *Okay*, she thought, *not checking the times of the pictures was dumb, but in the end the times were irrelevant. It did not matter when the pictures were taken. It was him!* She was sure of it. Even if the facial recognition software was not 100 percent sure, she was. She realized she was still holding the box of donuts. She dropped the box off on the break room table.

Back at her desk, she busied herself with the Bravo file, but continued to think about the data. There are things software do not catch: mannerisms, attitudes... gut feelings. That was it. It was her gut, the elusive feeling the old-timers always talked about, the deep-down knowledge that you were right, no matter how much the evidence pointed the other way.

The old-timers in the Agency would not let something like that slide. They would pursue every avenue, every possible reason ... and maybe, even some impossible reasons. She stopped, and found herself at the big window overlooking the parking lot. She stared out at the grey asphalt, the green surrounding woods, and the blue sky beyond. *How would the old-timers handle something like this?* she wondered.

Impossible reasons... That word kept coming up in her mind. It was *impossible* for Bailey to have been in two places at practically the same time. It was *impossible* for him to go around the world in a day. But... what if it was possible? Somehow, some way she had not thought of. What if he could do it?

Realizing she still had a 10 AM deadline, Tabitha buried herself in the Columbian report. After the drug cartels broke up in the 1990's, control over the production of cocaine shifted to various paramilitary groups. All the former drug lords in Columbia were either killed or in prison... except one. Valentin Bravo managed to avoid the purge by building his own private army: *Depredator*, the Predators, led by a man called El Gancho. The CIA and the

State Department regularly shared intelligence on *Depredador* with the Columbian government, specifically General Tomar Gomez, the head of their anti-drug operation. Tabitha pulled up the most recent intel and collected it in a file for Weaver... But she couldn't stop thinking about Bailey.

She decided she needed to talk to someone about it. Someone outside the Agency, someone independent. She had muddied her own waters enough already. There was no way she would mention Bailey again inside the Agency until she had absolute proof of... whatever it was that was going on.

The bell over the door jingled as Tabitha entered. To her left were racks of magazines and comic books. Movie posters and bookshelves lined the walls. A bulletin board announced upcoming science fiction conventions. Tiny tanks and rows of miniature soldiers stood patiently on a tabletop battlefield. A ceiling fan circled silently overhead. She smelled burnt popcorn. Tabitha sighed as she looked over her shoulder, hoping nobody she knew saw her enter the comics shop.

"Can I help you?" asked a man to her right. He had shoulder-length hair hanging from a bright bald spot on top of his head. His full beard had specks of popcorn, as did his Star Wars t-shirt. He sat in a tattered recliner lounge chair, a DVD of some Japanese anime in his hand.

"I... was looking for some advice," Tabitha said, not sure how to start. "I'm a... writer, and I'm doing research for a story."

"Ah," said the man. "Fanfic, or original?"

"Um," said Tabitha, searching for the words, "well, it's about a man—I mean, a creature that can, well, be in two places at the same time."

"Sounds like a magical creature, like something from D & D," the man said, rising. He had trouble getting his enormous bulk out of the chair.

Tabitha had heard of D & D—the Dungeons and Dragons game—which had initially brought her to the comics shop. The man pulled a book off one of the shelves. "Or it could be a devil. D & D is full of devil creatures that can teleport from one place to another."

Tabitha's eyes lit up. "Yes," she said. "Something like that." The man opened the book. He flipped to a page with lists of different kinds of devils. He stopped at a page with a drawing of some kind of monster. Tabitha thought it looked like a gargoyle.

"Like this guy," the man pointed. Tabitha thought she smelled bubble gum on his breath. "The Pit Fiend can teleport. The Bone Devil can teleport and become invisible. Is that what you're looking for?"

"Yes, yes I think it is," Tabitha said. She opened her purse. "How much is this?"

She was on her lunch break, and stopped at a local fast food joint before heading back up the highway to Langley. Tabitha didn't want her colleagues see her looking through a silly game book. She flipped through the book while munching on a burger. The pictures of monsters and demons were colorful. She found the charts, directions and "initiative rolls" confusing, but something inside her told her she was on the right track.

Teleportation. It was the only way to explain how Bailey could be in two different cities on the same day. According to the character statistics in the book, players could also use a talisman or some sort of magical device to travel from one place to another. It seemed impossible—but she recalled reading a scientific journal where scientists had been working on digitally reducing objects to light waves and reconstruction them elsewhere. It sounded like something from science fiction—or fantasy, she reminded herself—but perhaps Bailey had access to some device that—

Tabitha stopped. She took a deep breath and closed the book. What the hell was she thinking? This was not some fantasy wargaming world, this was not some science fiction TV show, this was real life, and in real life people did not teleport. It could not happen. It was impossible. End of story.

Tabitha put the burger down. She had been wrong about Bailey. She had been wrong about everything. The pictures were some sort of coincidence, the resemblances to Bailey a fluke of happenstance, the partial fingerprint simple human error. It was all a dead end. Magic and fantasy had no place in her reality-centerd world of international intelligence. Every second she dwelled on it just made her look more foolish. She stood and went back to her car, leaving the book and the half-eaten hamburger on the table. She was no longer hungry.

THE SPOOK

CHAPTER 11 –THURSDAY AFTERNOON

An internal email popped up as soon as Tabitha got back to work. Someone named Benton in Forensics had something for her to pick up right away. *The hell?* She thought. Tabitha grabbed a donut from the break room on her way to the elevator.

Forensics was on the third floor, an internal area with no windows. Tabitha's ID badge beeped on the scanner and the door unlocked. Inside, she found herself at a long, very clean counter. A pretty, young redheaded girl greeted her with a smile. "Hello!" she said cheerfully. "How can I help you?"

"Agent Benton said he had something for me," she said, holding up her ID. "I'm Tabitha Van Brunt."

"Right!" the redhead said, her eyes scanning below the counter. "Ah, here it is." The girl pulled out a large package wrapped in a plastic evidence bag. She slid it across the counter and produced a clipboard with papers. "Sign here, please."

"Hold it, wait, what is this?" Tabitha said. "What am I signing for?"

The redhead retrieved the clipboard and read the papers. "Processed items from Hartford, Pennsylvania raid," she read, along with the date. The girl pointed to the signature on the order, which read Conrad.

Tabitha sighed. Very funny, Conrad, she thought. It was the stuff the Company had taken from Bailey's house to test. "Okay, fine," she said, signing the papers. The redhead took the clipboard, stapled some pages together and placed them on top of the package. The clerk handed over a receipt.

"Have a nice day!" she said smiling.

"Yeah, right," Tabitha said, stuffing the papers into her pocket. She put the bundle under her arm and left. Back on her own floor, she looked at the bag with curiosity. A passing conference room was empty, so she stepped inside. Tabitha laid the bag down and began pulling the contents out, spreading them across the long table.

The black BDU shirt was there, as was a pair of army boots. The fingerless gloves were in a separate, smaller bag.

Tabitha thought about it for another minute, then put everything back into the big evidence bag. At her desk, she logged off her computer, scooped up the files she was working on, then waved to the receptionist. "I'm taking some personal time," she said, heading for the elevator.

The app on Tabitha's phone said she should have been able to make the trip to Harrisburg in just over two hours. Traffic and an accident on Highway 15 made it more like three. She pulled into Harrisburg at half past 5 PM. She knew Bailey's address from the warrant, and navigated the streets of Colonial Park before pulling up in front of a small, white brick house. Every house on the street looked exactly the same.

The yard was well-tended, but she noticed skid marks in the driveway. A trash can sat next to the curb. As she climbed out of her car, she spotted Bailey walking around from the side of the house. He was carrying a rake, and stopped when he spotted her. Tabitha picked up the evidence bag and walked around to the sidewalk.

"Hello," she said. "We—um, I wanted to return your things to you."

Bailey said nothing, then walked down the short slope to the sidewalk. He leaned the rake against the mailbox. "Your guys made a mess in my house. The neighbors got pretty worked up."

Tabitha sighed. "I'm sorry about that." She handed over the package. "It was all my fault, a big misunderstanding."

Bailey looked at the package before balancing it on top of the mailbox. "I guess you guys were just doing your job. At least nothing was broken." He frowned as he tried to read her expression. "You said it was your fault. Did you get in trouble or something?"

Tabitha exhaled, shaking her head. "My boss is chalking the whole thing up to 'experience.' All the photos and records and that stupid fingerprint... I guess I got carried away."

Bailey's expression softened. He leaned his hand on the mailbox post. "So, are you a spy?"

"Me? No, I'm a photo analyst. Not everybody in the CIA is a super spy. I'm in a little over my head here, to be honest. I'm really sorry to put you through all this." Tabitha reached into a pocket and pulled out a tiny wallet. She pulled out a business card.

"Look," she said, handing it across to Bailey, "If there is anything we—that, is, I—can do to make it up to you, please let me know." The words were clumsy, but she hoped the sincerity made up for them.

Bailey reached out over the roof of the car. He took the card and read it. "Okay," he said. "Thanks."

Tabitha felt a sense of relief. She managed a smile as she got back in her car and drove away down the narrow street. She could see him in her rear-view mirror: a normal, average guy, standing in his yard beside his mailbox, watching her leave. A simple, ordinary man.

THE SPOOK

CHAPTER 12 – THURSDAY EVENING

The sun was low in the west, sky a ruddy blue as the day shifted into twilight. Overhead, a cargo jetliner roared into the sky. A light breeze blew in off the Caribbean. The thump of machinery drifted in over the water. A freighter lingered due north on the hazy horizon. The Seagulls lingered on the water's edge.

Puerto Bolivar was established in 1982 and soon became Columbia's biggest port. It was the largest exporter of coal in Latin America. The port had rail lines, roads and an airport, making it a vital transport hub for the country. Columbian customs officials were stretched thin maintaining control over smuggling in the port.

The man in the black shirt checked his watch. The deserted road ahead led to a jetty, poking out into the water. To his left, two huge oil tanks loomed over the road, gentle waves lapping at the beach down the slope. The ocean breeze masked a lingering scent of oil. A junkyard surrounded by a low wall of old tires lay up the road. He could see an intersection back up past the junkyard. He started walking towards it, his boots crunching on the loose asphalt. The collar of his black shirt flapped up as it saluted the wind.

He had only walked a hundred yards when a vehicle appeared on the road ahead. The man quickly got off the road and stood in the shade of some scrub trees next to the wall of tires. As it approached, he noticed another vehicle parked next to a shack inside the junkyard. From the silhouette, the stranger could see it was a dark-colored, four-door sports utility vehicle. A large, husky man stood nearby with a shotgun. The vehicle approached, another SUV, this one cream-colored, and it scattered gravel into the ditches as it turned into the junkyard.

The engine stopped and all the doors opened. He heard shouting and moved down the wall of old tires to get a better look. Figures were emerging from the SUV. More shouts. A figure stumbled out from behind the first vehicle. He was bare-chested, and had his hands tied in front of him. The man had a bad feeling something terrible was about to happen.

Another man appeared from behind the dark vehicle. He wore a red shirt, and had a rope in his hands. He looped it around the first man's neck and used it to bring the man to his knees. There was bruising on the bound man's head and torso. "Stay down!" the second man said in English.

A third man appeared. A small cloud of cigar smoke swirled as he closed the door behind him. He seemed to be taking his time. He stepped forward and stood before the kneeling man. "Shamoun," said the smoking man. "Shamoun, you have been very sloppy in your work. El Marinero does not appreciate loose ends."

"I know, I know," pleaded the bound Shamoun. "Please, my friend Gancho, please give me another chance!"

The one called Gancho shook his head. "I am afraid I cannot do that, my friend. You had specific orders to ship the Shinzhen product to Cairo. Instead, you had it flown here. El Marinero does not appreciate disobedience."

"I... I thought this was where he wanted the product to go, mi amigo, so that he could see for himself. I meant no harm, por favor!"

"The product is supposed to be kept under thirty-nine degrees and you bring it to a tropical country!" El Gancho cried. "What were you thinking?"

"Please, senor, just give me another chance," whimpered Shamoun.

Gancho shook his head. "It is not only your stupidity, but it is bad business to let disobedience slide. We must make an example of you. You... and those that love you. Alinearlos!" There was a commotion behind the truck. The man in black could see dust being kicked up from the gravel road. Several figures were slowly coming forward.

The man called Shamoun started crying as four figures were brought into the dusty light: a woman, her arms bound behind her, pushed along by shadowy armed figures. The woman let out a cry, and Shamoun struggled against the rope looped around his neck, trying to reach out to her. The woman's face was streaked with tears. The man gasped as a second thug brought out a young boy, maybe eight or nine years old. The boy broke away from the thug and ran to the woman, wrapping his arms around her waist. Shamoun was shouting something to her in Arabic. At the far end of the junkyard, the shadowy figures pushed her and the boy against the wall of tires, and then backed away. "The slate must be wiped clean, senor," Gancho said.

Oh no! the man thought. He started to shout, but just then a burst of automatic gunfire rang out. The woman and boy shuddered under the hail of bullets, then crumpled to the ground. Shamoun wailed in profound grief and squirmed on the ground, trying to reach his wife and son, but the man in the red shirt held him back, forcing him to watch the horrible spectacle. Two of the figures fired their guns into the air and cheered.

The one called Gancho turned to the despairing Shamoun. He threw his cigar away and stepped forward, staring down at the bound man. From his belt, he drew something curved and metal—a hook, the man realized. He reared back to strike the prone man—

"No!" cried the man in black, horrified by the sight. He was on his feet before he realized it.

The group on the road turned as one towards him. His appearance seemed to make no sense to them. Framed in tumbled-down spot in the wall of tires stood a gringo, wearing a black shirt. They all just stared at him.

The man suddenly realized how vulnerable he was.

"Lanzamiento!" cried Gancho. "Shoot! Shoot!"

The man in black turned and dove behind the tires as the junkyard lit up with gunfire. He hit the dirt just as a deadly rain of lead scattered leaves from the scrubby tree. He could hear the bullets thumping into and through the stacks of tires. His face was flat against the oily ground. His heartbeat drummed loud against his temples. They were coming! He quickly crawled on all fours along the wall, keeping low, rushing as fast as he could go. He moved towards the far corner of the wall.

He turned and saw shadows emerge from the junkyard entrance. He ducked around the corner. At a break between stacks of tires, he could see into the yard. The one called Shamoun, still on his knees, was crying out in agony and despair. Beside him, Gancho turned to the sound, as if noticing Shamoun for the first time. He looked at the hay hook in his hand. With all the shouting and gunshots, there would be no time for him to enjoy himself. He transferred the hook to his left hand and drew an automatic pistol from his waistband.

Gancho casually placed his gun against Shamoun's head and fired again. The impact created a small cloud of blood and gore as the man's dead body slumped to the ground. "No witnesses!" he could hear Benito yell.

The man looked around. Beyond the walled junkyard, there was only empty slope down to the beach. The empty road offered no cover, no place to hide. He turned and rushed down the wall towards the water, hoping for a space beyond the next corner.

He stopped to look back. Two men were up on the road. He could hear shouting. The loose rocks under his feet sounded like an avalanche in the gathering gloom. Did they think he took off down the road, towards the jetty? He rushed towards the water.

"Hey!" came a cry to his left.

There was a clap of thunder—and something struck him in the side, just above the belt line. He smelled something hot just as his eyes registered a flash of light. All the air left his lungs; his legs seemed suddenly weak. The ground fell away beneath him, and he found himself slipping down the filthy wall of tires. Somehow, he got one knee up, and found enough footing to duck around the far corner of the tire wall. Far off in the distance he could hear shouts, the sound of people running.

His mouth was suddenly very dry. He tried to move, but felt stuck to the soft ground. His eyes could still see the light flash, blinking up at the starry sky. He thought of that time when he was ten years old, when his parents were in Washington D.C. for the Fourth of July. They had picnicked on the National Mall, and when darkness came the most amazing fireworks display erupted high above them: the colorful explosions lit up the sky.

He could hear footsteps getting closer. Something vibrated near his hand... It was the alarm on his wrist watch going off. The man felt a sense of relief as a flashlight beam hit the plants hovering over him. He thought of hot dogs, the scent of fresh-cut grass, and fireworks....

Two gunmen approached the wall of old tires. The one in the red shirt was in front, rifle in hand, raised, stock to his shoulder, ready to fire again. He had long, dark hair, tied back in a pony tail. The other was shorter and had a .45 automatic in one hand, a flashlight in the other. They were following the footprints in the gravely earth. The one with the rifle motioned for the other to move in closer. Ten feet away from the corner they aimed their weapons and moved forward to find...

Nothing. The wall of tires extended along the shoreline to the rear of the junkyard shack. The space in front of them was empty. The flashlight beam showed no footprints. "He's gone!" cried the one with the rifle. The other scanned the surface of the bay with his flashlight.

The shorter one squinted out onto the dark waters of the bay. "I saw him fall. Where did he go?" The one in the red shirt brought up his rifle and fired a half dozen rounds into the waters beyond.

The shorter one turned his flashlight beam on the ground. "Look! Blood! The trail runs around the corner and then... stops." He gasped in horror. "A witch!" he whispered, crossing himself. "Madre dios! The earth itself has swallowed him up!"

"Shut up!" said Benito. "Shine that light over here!" The beam of light went back and forth across the water. Benito lowered his rifle and looked down at the blood trail. "He was a man, amigo," Benito said. "Witches do not bleed."

"But... where did he go?"

"He must be dead," the one called Benito concluded, shouldering his weapon. "If he swam out into the bay, he will not survive the night. No point wasting any more time out here." Benito and his friend went back towards the road. The two walked back through the foliage, their trousers damp from early dew.

The one called Gancho stood by the SUV, hands on hips. "Well?"

"He is dead, El Gancho," said Benito. He shot a threatening sidelong glance at his friend, who remained silent.

"Excellent," said El Gancho. He turned to the SUV. "Time to go."

THE SPOOK

El Gancho and the others climbed into the vehicles and drove away into the darkening night. Above, stars had already appeared in the sky.

CHAPTER 13 – EARLY FRIDAY, WASHINGTON D.C.

The two officers walked down the dark concrete path, night sticks in hand. To their left, traffic was busy even at that late hour. Behind them, great white buildings led off into the distance. The air was cool, without a breath of wind. "What sounds good?" the first one asked.

"Chicken," said the second. "A big bucket of chicken. With coleslaw and corn on the cob."

"Biscuits and gravy?"

"You got it," the second officer said. "Dibs on the wings. I'm starting to get hungry now..." The first officer had stopped, and was shining his flashlight out onto the grass. "What? What is it?"

The flashlight beam fell on a lone figure, lying motionless in the grass. "Oh, my God," said the first officer. He rushed over to the man's side and knelt down. The second officer followed, his flashlight finding a man, flat on his back, his clothes soaked in blood.

"Is he alive?" said the second officer. The first one nodded his head.

"Looks like he's been shot!" said the first officer, applying pressure on the wound. "There's blood everywhere. Call for an ambulance!"

The second officer checked the man's pulse as he pulled out his radio with the other hand. The pulse was weak. "Dispatch, this is Dugan. I've got a man down just off 17th Street, near Constitution Avenue. Request ambulance."

The first officer leaned forward to look at the man's face. The man's eyelids were heavy, and his breathing was ragged. He kept blinking his eyes. "Stay with me, buddy," he said. "Help's on the way."

Paramedics arrived within minutes. The second officer left the man's side to flag down the ambulance. The paramedics went to work on the man immediately. Red and white lights flashed up and down the street. As soon as the man was stabilized, the paramedics loaded the man onto a board and strapped him down. An oxygen mask was placed over his mouth. They would transfer him to a gurney once they got him to the ambulance.

As they carried him across the grassy expanse, the man opened his eyes and looked up. Towering above them all, the clean, straight lines of the brightly lit spire dominated the scene.

Bailey managed a smile. The Washington Monument was exactly as he remembered it...

The cellphone was vibrating loudly on Tabitha's nightstand, dancing its way to the edge before her hand rescued it. She rolled back onto the pillow and answered it with her eyes closed. "Hello?"

"Ms. Van Brunt?" came a woman's voice. "Langley switchboard. I'm transferring a call to you. Stand by for D.C. Police."

Tabitha opened her eyes. "What?" The phone clicked as she sat up in bed. The clock radio read 4:05.

"Hello? Tabitha Van Brunt?" came a man's voice.

Tabitha frowned in confusion. "I'm... Hello?"

"Is this Tabitha Van Brunt?" the voice repeated, in a firmer tone.

"Yes," she replied. "Who's this?"

"Ma'am, this is Sergeant Tripp of the DCPD," came the reply.

She still didn't know what was going on. "What can I do for you, officer?"

"Ma'am, your name came up in the investigation of an assault on the National Mall late last night," Tripp said.

"An assault?" repeated Tabitha. "How did my name come up?"

"That's what I'd like to talk to you about, ma'am," Tripp said. "Have you recently been the victim of a crime?"

"Of course not," she replied.

"Do you live in Washington proper?"

"No, I'm across the river," Tabitha said. "I don't understand—"

"Ma'am," interrupted Tripp, "would it be possible for you to come to George Washington University Hospital? That's where I am now. It could really help us clear things up."

"What, you mean, now?" Tabitha said. "I have work in the morning."

"Employers usually understand about these things, ma'am," Tripp said. "And you'd be helping out in a criminal investigation."

Tabitha stopped for a moment. The officer knew who her employer was; the call was routed to her from CIA headquarters. "Ma'am?" Tripp was asking.

Tabitha looked at her nightstand clock again. "Okay, okay," she said. "So long as we make it quick. You said George Washington University Hospital?"

"Yes, ma'am," said the officer. "Just go to the emergency room. We'll be there."

"Fine," sighed Tabitha. She disconnected and set the phone back on the nightstand. She shook her head. What was going on? Looking back at her phone, she thought about sending her supervisor a text—but there was no point waking him up until she had more information.

From her Yorktown apartment, it was a short drive across the river to Washington Hospital, but Tabitha still had to put up with early morning traffic. The hospital was four blocks from the White House, in the middle of town. She parked her car in the lot and walked around to the emergency room. Dressed in sweats and sneakers, she did not care what she looked like.

The automatic doors opened for her as she walked inside the medical center. Through a short corridor, she found the waiting room. At first, there seemed to be no one there, but then a nurse walked past a doorway. From around a corner, a uniformed police officer appeared. "Ah," he said, "Ms. Van Brunt? I'm Sgt. Tripp." He held out his hand and shook hers.

"What's this all about?" Tabitha said.

"This should only take a minute, ma'am," the servant said. "I appreciate you coming over like this." Down a hallway, a doctor in pale blue scrubs walked out of a doorway carrying a clipboard.

"Doctor," the officer said, getting the doctor's attention. "This is the person I told you about. Could you tell her about your patient?"

"Certainly," the doctor said. He held out his hand. "Dr.

Quarry. The officer told you we had an assault patient this morning?" She shook his hand.

"That's all I was told," Tabitha said, her annoyance growing. The doctor looked at Tripp.

"Ma'am," the officer said, "last night, officers on the mall found an injured man. It looked like he'd been robbed and assaulted. They brought him in here a couple of hours ago. No ID, no wallet or keys, he looked like a typical robbery victim."

"We treated him for what looked like a gunshot wound," the doctor said as he led them into an examination room. "We get a lot of gunshot wounds here, as you might imagine, so we know what we're looking at."

"Yeah, so?" Tabitha said impatiently.

The doctor picked up a sheet of x-ray film and slapped it up onto an exam light. He flipped the switch and the light flickered on. "The man had a series of wounds along his left side consistent with a shotgun wound. We got to looking at his x-rays, and we noticed something missing."

Tabitha was starting to get exasperated. "Missing? Missing what?"

"Buckshot." The x-ray displayed before them showed a normal human chest. Tabitha had seen x-rays of gunshot victims before, where the metal bullet was clearly visible on the screen. There was clearly no bullet in that image.

"The pattern from his rib cage to his left hip looks like a shotgun wound from long range," the doctor continued, "but whatever entered his body had simply disappeared. There's also major bruising on his left floating rib, like something grazed it. Whatever it was didn't go deep enough to damage his internal organs. I've got him patched up and on massive antibiotics right now."

On a certain level, Tabitha was intrigued. She shook her head. "As interesting as that is, what does any of this have to do with me?"

"Well," interjected the officer, "when all that came up, I decided to take a second look at his clothes." The officer went to a large manila envelope sitting on an opposite table. "Maybe see if there was something we missed. And there was." He reached inside the manila envelope and pulled out a sealed, clear plastic bag. "We found this," he said, handing it to Tabitha. She turned the bag over, and gasped. Inside the evidence bag was a business card.

Her business card.

"Ma'am," said the officer slowly, "is this going to be a matter of national security? Something we need to get your bosses involved with?" Tabitha's mind raced. Just the idea of something belonging to her appearing at a crime scene was shocking.

"I don't know," she said finally. "Maybe."

"When I saw these wounds," the doctor said, tapping his finger on the x-ray, "I thought of those spy stories from the 1960's, about ice bullets and stuff like that." He pointed to the x-ray. "And now here you are with the CIA... Is this some sort of secret spy assassination weapon?"

"I have to wonder," the officer added, "ma'am, if he's some international spy, if this might be an assassination disguised as a botched robbery."

Tabitha held up her hands. "Hold it right there," she said. "Whatever this is—I'm sure it's for somebody way above my pay grade to say. I'm just an analyst."

"So was Jack Ryan," muttered Tripp.

Tabitha frowned at him. She'd gotten enough Tom Clancy jokes from her family when she joined the CIA, and none of them were that funny. She looked at the card again, and realized she'd only ever given out a handful of them, mostly to family. "Hold on. Who is it? Is he okay?"

"He's in recovery," said Dr. Quarry. "He'll be fine. So far, however, he hasn't been very cooperative about his identity."

"The kind of thing you'd expect from a spy," added Tripp.

Tabitha shook her head. She started to say something— "Oh!"

"What is it?" Tripp asked.

"LeBlanc. Paul LeBlanc," she said in low tones. "He's from Interpol— I just met him a couple of days ago. I can't remember if I gave him a card or not ... This could be a national security issue after all."

"Let's go see him," Tripp said. "Maybe he'll talk to you. This could still be a simple case of robbery-assault."

"Where is he?" she asked.

"Recovery room three," Dr. Quarry said, and started leading the way. I had him moved to a private room when they found your card."

Tabitha followed the doctor, her mind racing. If LeBlanc had been assaulted, she would have to contact the State Department immediately. The French Embassy and Interpol would have to be called... she hoped she hadn't found herself in the middle of an international incident.

"He didn't tell you who he was?" Tabitha asked as they walked.

"Well," said the officer, "he was still pretty groggy from the pain medication when I talked to him."

The doctor led Tabitha and the officer down a hallway and around a corner. Ahead, a nurse was standing in the doorway of a hospital room. Her back was to them as they approached, blocking the doorway.

"... the doctor will explain everything to you," the nurse was saying.

"What's the matter, nurse?" Dr. Quarry asked.

The nurse turned around. She was in her late thirties, and had a tired look in her eyes. It was probably getting towards the end of her shift. "Your patient is getting a little anxious." She stepped to the side of the doorway to let the doctor pass.

"I've got to get out of here!" came a voice from inside the room.

Tabitha froze in her tracks. She had been expecting LeBlanc's French accent, but this voice was different— The breath seemed to catch in her lungs. That was not LeBlanc's voice. It was Bailey's voice! She recognized it from talking to him before. And she had given him a card. What was Bailey doing here?

Just then, a patient in a hospital gown came up from Tabitha's left. He was walking with an IV stand, rolling it along. Tabitha realized she was in his way. "Excuse me," she said, stepping out of the way.

Tripp and the doctor turned when she spoke, then stepped forward into the room. Tabitha could see the foot of the bed through the doorway as the doctor came to a halt and looked around.

"Nurse?" called the doctor. "Where's my patient?"

The nurse was still standing at the doorway. "What?" she asked. "He's right—" the nurse's voice stopped. Tabitha followed the nurse into the room. The doctor and the officer were both standing at the foot of the bed. The empty bed. The sheets were disrupted, dotted with blood stains, but that was all.

The nurse stared at the empty bed. "Where'd he go?" she asked.

Tabitha stood behind the nurse and looked around the room. It was a windowless, interior room with nowhere to go. The cut-up remains of a black shirt were in a wastebasket. Officer Tripp bent down to look under the bed. The nurse turned to look inside the small lavatory. The doctor was looking behind the head of the bed... And just then, Tabitha noticed the rolling nightstand, pushed up against the wall. There was an unwrapped plastic cup, a small plastic water pitcher, and a watch. A plain analog wrist watch with a leather band.

There was no one under the bed. Tripp looked up just as Tabitha was leaving the room. "Just a minute," Tripp called out.

In the hallway, Tripp caught up with Tabitha. "Look, I don't know where he went, but he was right in there. I'm sure you heard him."

"Officer," said Tabitha, adjusting her hair, "whoever it is, or was, I have no idea how they got my business card. And I doubt this has anything to do with national security. Now if you'll excuse me, I have to go."

Tripp started to say something, but his voice fell mute as he watched her walk down the hallway and out of view.

Tabitha walked straight to her car. She got in, started the engine, and pulled out of the parking lot, staring straight ahead the whole time. She got on the expressway, and did not stop until she was in her apartment complex parking lot. There, she parked and shut off the engine.

She took a deep breath, and reached into her coat pocket. Tabitha almost felt her heart stop. It was still there. She pulled out the watch and looked at it. It was a simple analog mainspring wrist watch, with a face numbered 1 to 12. The crystal looked scratched. She realized it was not just an old watch—it was an antique. On the back, something had once been engraved, but the words had long since been rubbed away. She looked at the strap again. If there had been any doubt in her mind, it faded away. She was absolutely certain it was the same watch Bailey had worn in the library earlier that week. The same one he wore talking in his front yard.

It was him. She'd heard his voice. She had his watch. It was him.

Back inside her apartment, there was no use going back to bed. Tabitha showered, dressed, picked up a breakfast sandwich from a fast-food restaurant and drove in to work. The sun was just coming up when she arrived at CIA headquarters. The security guard at the gate was surprised to see her.

"Starting your day a little early, aren't you?' he smiled.

"Working towards early retirement, Frank," she replied.

Once she got to her office, however, she wasn't sure what to do next. The notes from the Harrisburg raid had the phone number for the library, Bailey's home address, but not his home phone number. She could look it up... but anything she did would leave a trail on her computer. Tabitha pulled out her cellphone and punched in the numbers for the Eisenhower Public Library and started to call—but of course, it would be closed that time of day. She saved the number.

Weaver appeared down the hallway. "Morning," he called before disappearing around a corner.

Tabitha waved and put the phone down, setting it aside, her movements slow and deliberate, like her phone was a bomb that might go off at any time. She took a deep breath, and tried to focus on work. Should she tell her boss about the hospital? Should she file a report? Except for the watch, she had no proof anything had happened. She was already on thin ice after the Harrisburg debacle; one more mistake and she might find herself serving lunch in the cafeteria.

She busied herself with her most recent assignments, going over reports, making phone calls, getting a cup of coffee... but her eyes kept going back to her phone. It was almost 10 AM when she decided everything must be open in Harrisburg. After casually walking to the restroom and checking to see she was alone, she called the library.

"Eisenhower Public Library," came a chipper female voice.

"James Bailey, please," Tabitha asked.

"I'm sorry," the voice said. "He called in sick today. He

said he might be out for a couple of days."

"Oh," Tabitha replied. "Nothing... serious, I hope?" *Like a gunshot wound?*

"He didn't say."

"Well, um," she thought quickly, "this is the loan agency. I have the figures for his credit rating and I thought he'd want them right away. Do you have his home number handy?"

"Yeah, sure," the voice replied. "Hang on." After a few moments the voice read off a series of numbers. Tabitha quickly wrote them down on her wrist.

"Thank you," Tabitha said, and hung up. *Out sick. Getting shot in the chest will do that to you,* Tabitha thought. But who shot him? How could he disappear like that? If he could move like that, he could easily be across the world in a few hours.

It was impossible. Except... she reached into her coat pocket, and felt the watch. That was the proof. It had to be him. Right then, another woman came into the rest room, so Tabitha went back to her desk. In between reports, she punched Bailey's home number into her cellphone. It was mid-afternoon when she finally got a break. She went outside to the courtyard, looked to confirm she was alone, and called Bailey's home.

The phone rang once, twice, three times—then a click. "Hello."

The exact same voice as in the hospital! Tabitha drew her breath to speak, but then the voice continued, "I can't come to the phone right now. Please leave your message after the beep."

Voice mail. She looked at her phone, the critical moment suddenly anticlimactic. The line beeped. Tabitha could think of nothing to say, certainly nothing that would fit in a voice mail message, so she disconnected.

Tabitha walked back up to her cubicle. She tapped her feet in excitement. She could not sit still. She had to get up and walk a circuit around the floor. She got herself another cup of coffee, completely forgetting about the cup she already had at her desk.

It was him, she thought... and I can't tell anybody. Because it's crazy. Anything I say will sound crazy. She took her older cup of coffee back to the lounge and poured it down the sink.

It's insane. People can't do that. People can't teleport, be in two places hundreds of miles apart. It's impossible. And yet...

Her hand felt the watch still in her pocket. She had to do something.

Her work load kept her from even thinking about it the rest of the day. The Balkan situation became more crucial, and she was on the Internet most of the afternoon checking sources and verifying quotes. A militia group had suddenly emerged, and several sources wanted more information. Satellite photos showed highway traffic in Kosovo had increased dramatically. A report came through of some Chinese arms loose on the black market, but the trail led towards the Philippines. Jones, an analyst from another division, was in and out of her office all day, checking on troop movements. It was an exhausting day. She did not realize how late in the day it was until she passed a window and saw how dark it had gotten outside.

The current crisis resolved, Tabitha sat back in her chair... and looked at her cell phone. It sat on her desk next to the computer monitor. Looking over her shoulder, to be sure nobody was watching, she took the watch out of her pocket and laid it on her desk. The leather strap was smooth to the touch.

The crumpled papers on the edge of her desk drew her attention. It was the preliminary report from the search on Bailey's home. Tabitha had forgotten all about it when she picked up his boots. The first page described the house and furniture. The second page listed contents of his closets and garage: very standard stuff. There was a photo of his living room: couch, chair, TV and bookcases. One shelf was full of narrow, yellow volumes. *Old issues of National Geographic*, the caption on the back read. *Well,* she thought, *everybody must collect something.* There were several coffee table books of famous places and landmarks across the world.

The last page was the forensics report on the confiscated clothes. The lab found traces of sand and grass on the boots, and there was soot in the fingerless gloves, all of indeterminate origin. They also found a hair on the BDU shirt that came from an African lion, of all things. Strange, but nothing illegal.

Tabitha returned to the restroom, and made sure she was alone. She took a deep breath and blew it out. Gingerly, she pulled out her phone and dialed the number. One ring. Two rings. Then a click.

"Hello?"

Tabitha swallowed. "Mr. Bailey? This is Tabitha Van Brunt, from the CIA. We—"

Click. He hung up.

Tabitha ran her fingers through her hair. She hit redial.

Three rings, then: "What do you want?"

"This isn't an official call," she said in a rush. "It's just me." Silence. She decided to take a chance. "I found a watch at the hospital this morning. I thought you might like to talk about it. Or, maybe, just somebody to talk to." She waited for a response. "Mr. Bailey?"

She thought she heard a sigh on the other end. Then, "Do you know where the Korean War Memorial is?"

It seemed like an odd question. "Yes, of course."

Another pause. "Eight PM." The line went dead.

THE SPOOK

CHAPTER 14 – FRIDAY

The lights were on at the San Cordero mansion when the two vehicles pulled up to the front gate. The guard waved them through when he saw El Gancho. Before they even got to the front steps, they could see the transport truck parked at the far end of the estate.

"Mierda!" spat El Gancho. "What was that idiot thinking? Hijo de puta!"

"What are we going to do?" asked Benito.

"We—" El Gancho suddenly stopped as he gazed off towards the docks. A beautiful speedboat was pulling up to shore, a boat he recognized. The SUV came to a halt, and as El Gancho climbed out of the vehicle his cellphone buzzed. He frowned at the screen before answering.

"Yes, Senor Johnson."

"Gancho. Is everything on track for Chiro shipment?"

Gancho glanced at the truck, looked at Estiban for a long moment, then replied in a cheerful tone of voice: "Everything is in order, Senor." Johnson hung up without replying. At the dock, the two of them could see Bravo climbing out of the speedboat. He turned to help his little girl out onto the dock. Gancho watched as Juan trotted down the dock towards the boat.

"Senor Bravo!" he called. "I hope you and little Maria enjoyed your boat ride."

"Indeed we did, Juan," Bravo replied. "But I am afraid I have kept my little one out past her suppertime."

"Not to worry, senor," Juan said. "Consuelo has kept everything warm for you." He held his hand out to the little girl. "Come, little one, let us get you some supper!" Bravo watched his daughter walk up to the main house, smiling with pride. Gancho saw the smile fade when El Marinaro spotted the old truck parked next to his big garage.

"Wait here," Gancho said to Estiban as he walked to meet Bravo at the grassy shore. Lights had come on in the main house, sending a warm, golden glow into the darkening twilight.

"Mi amigo," Bravo greeted, not sounding friendly, "what is this eyesore doing on my property?" He nodded towards the truck.

"Because it is your property, senor," Gancho said cheerfully. "Courtesy of Senor Johnson, it is the investment he had transported from China."

"The baby gas?" Bravo said. "What the hell is it doing here? Johnson said it was supposed to go to Egypt for processing."

"It was Shamoun, senor," Gancho said. "A selfish attempt on his part to ingratiate himself in your good graces."

The older man frowned. "I do not suffer fools, amigo," Bravo said. "I want him removed immediately."

Gancho raised his hands. "He has already been dealt with, senor," he said. "Along with any complications from future generations."

Bravo nodded approvingly. "Good man," he said, patting Gancho on the arm. "I can always count on you to expedite such matters."

"I try my best, senor," Gancho said, bowing his head in respect.

Bravo looked at the truck again and cleared his throat. "But we cannot have such a monstrosity within sight of the house. Have it moved to the bunkhouse until we can find suitable transport."

"Right away, senor," Gancho said. He waved to Estiban, who took off at a brisk walk towards the truck. He waved to Bravo as the older man walked towards the house. "Buenos noches, senor."

Gancho stood at the edge of the dock until he heard the truck's engine turn over. He walked to the gravel drive and met the truck as it came around. Estiban stopped the vehicle and leaned out the window. Gancho glanced around to be sure no one was within earshot.

"Take the truck to the bunkhouse. And contact our friend at the *parlamento*," he said over the rumble of the idling engine. "I want him to arrange a confidential meeting."

"All right," Estiban said. "A meeting with whom?"

Gancho looked Estiban in the eye and silently mouthed the name with his lips.

"Joder!" Estiban breathed. "Are you insane? Why?"

Gancho patted the side of the truck. "Because opportunity beckons, my friend. And we must grab it by the *cojones*!"

THE SPOOK

CHAPTER 15 – FRIDAY EVENING

Parking near the National Mall was a pain, as usual, but Tabitha found a space near the Smithsonian "castle," the museum's original home. It loomed overhead like a gothic cathedral as she made her way down the wide sidewalk.

Streetlights were starting to come on. Above, the Washington Monument shot straight up into the sky. She walked past it, towards the Lincoln Memorial, then turned up the path to the Korean Memorial.

Like many people, Tabitha found the memorial disturbing. She had seen it before, but never at dusk, as the shadows of early evening crept between the statues. The memorial had a group of figures, all walking up a short rise. The figures were supposed to illustrate soldiers making their way through a mine field, and the faces on the figures were anxious and taunt.

Tabitha walked through the memorial to the far wall. At first, the stone wall looks smudged and uneven. As she got closer, she saw the smudges were actually faces, laser-etched into the stone. The faces are designed to appear and disappear as you walked along the wall, illustrating the victims of war. It was like the victims of war were staring at you, wondering why you did not work harder to prevent such a tragedy. Tabitha always found the memorial to be a depressing place.

She turned—and there he was, standing behind one of the statues. Bailey was wearing a black hoodie, hands in pockets, blue jeans and black jogging shoes. He stood so still he almost blended into the figures etched on the stone wall. He studied her for a moment, the breeze ruffling his hair, then walked around the path to meet her, a slight limp in his gait. Her eyes never left his form. He stopped three feet from Tabitha.

Bailey held out an open hand. For a moment, Tabitha did not understand, then she reached into her pocket and pulled out the watch. She handed it to him. Without saying a word, he fastened it onto his wrist. With a twist of his fingers, he wound the watch. He gave her a long, hard look. His hands fell to his sides.

Bailey took a deep breath, then exhaled. He looked off across the expanse of the Mall. "I suppose you want an explanation."

She exhaled in frustration. "Hell—" she started, realizing her voice was loud and lowered it. "Hell yes, I want an explanation!"

Bailey nodded his head towards the Lincoln Memorial. "Let's go for a walk."

The sun had set, and the tourists had moved on to hotels. The Mall was empty, save for a few locals. A streetlight cast deep shadows on the Korean Memorial statues, stretching their features, making them look even sadder.

The two of them walked down the wide sidewalk. Tabitha did not know what to say. "That was you in the hospital, wasn't it? Somebody shot you?"

He held his side. Tabitha noticed he was taking careful steps as he walked. "They saw me," he said. "After they killed the family in the junkyard. They just shot them all. They didn't want any witnesses."

She stopped and stared. "Who got shot? Hold it, wait. Let's back up. How can you do... what you do?"

He shrugged his shoulders. "I don't know why it happened. I just... do."

"So, let me get this straight," she said. "You can, what, teleport? Anywhere?"

He shook his head. "I can only go places I've been before, or places I've seen pictures of. I have to have a really good idea of where I'm going."

"Ah," she said, thinking of the magazines in his house. The picture books. The National Geographics. "Just like that," she said. "Is it instantaneous?"

"Kinda, yeah," he replied. The smell of freshly-mowed grass drifted towards them. Ahead, a jogger started their way, then turned towards the World War II Memorial. Bailey touched his wounded side. He sighed deeply. "I guess I did need to talk to somebody after all. You're the first person I've told. I needed to tell somebody about, you know, what I can do, where I've been..."

"Where have you been?"

He shrugged his shoulders. "Pretty much everywhere. The Louvre, the North Pole, the Kremlin, the top of the Great Pyramid... that was all the first week, as soon as I got back from Afghanistan. I couldn't experiment much over there."

Tabitha shook her head. "How do you—that is, how does it work?"

He cocked his head to one side, searching for an answer. "It's kind of like flexing a nerve, wiggling your ears, something like that," he said. "It took a while to get it under control, to be sure I wouldn't do it in my sleep. That would be awkward." He stepped off the sidewalk to pick up an empty water bottle that had been tossed on the grass.

"When we talked to you in the library," she remembered, "when we showed you the pictures, you denied they were you."

Bailey cocked his head to one side. "Actually, no. If you want to get technical about it, I never flat-out denied anything."

Tabitha stopped in her tracks. She went over the conversation in her head. He was right. He had answered every question with another question, never specifically confirming or denying any of their allegations.

"Have you always been able to do this?"

He shook his head. "Something...happened to me in Afghanistan," he said. He started into the darkness. "It's hard to explain."

"What happened the first time you could teleport?"

"The first time, I thought I was dreaming. It freaked me out when I realized what happened, that it was real." Their footsteps echoed across the sidewalk.

"So," she said finally, searching for the words, "why aren't you rich? You could have gone inside Fort Knox, or some art museum. You could have filled your house with gold. Why haven't you teleported into all the world's banks and taken all their money?"

He frowned at her, like a parent looking at a child that had just said its first curse word. "That wouldn't be right, would it? That would be stealing."

"Well," she admitted, "yeah..."

He shook his head. "I couldn't do that. I'd never forgive myself."

"That was your fingerprint the Hong Kong police found, wasn't it?"

He shrugged. "I guess that was kind of sloppy, but I couldn't just let that guy bleed out in the street, could I?"

"So you weren't even trying to hide your fingerprints?"

"It's not like what I do is illegal," he replied. "I'm just helping out, wherever I can."

"Maybe not illegal," Tabitha said, "but certainly unorthodox. So why the gloves?"

He held out a bare hand. "They're just different enough to get people's attention. That's what people see, that's what they remember, not my face. Besides, you guys get plenty of convictions with palm prints. Without it, spy guys like you would've caught on to me long ago."

"Shouldn't you, I don't know, wear a mask or something?"

He turned to look at her. "Yeah, right, like a mask wouldn't attract any attention at all."

"And... and you never told anybody what you can do?"

He looked at her. "Would you? If you could pop anywhere in the world would you tell anybody? What do you think would happen if you did?"

"Well, I—"

"The government would snatch you up and try to duplicate you, turn you into a weapon, or crush you so you wouldn't become a weapon," Bailey said, answering his own question. "Or the CIA. You spy guys would make me a spook, sending me out to kill people or something."

"I'm not a spy," she insisted. "I just... okay, I work for spies." Tabitha felt defensive, but she knew he was right. "National security," she said to herself. "I know what my bosses would say. It would be too dangerous for the country to let you just run around free."

"Which is a pretty sad statement," he pointed out. "It's not like I can take anything with me when I wink out."

"What do you mean?"

"I'm still working it out," he said, stooping to pick up a crumpled fast-food wrapper. "But when I pop from one place to another, some stuff gets left behind. I can't take a cellphone, or a radio, or anything high-tech. Anything I wear has to be natural fibers, like cotton," he said, holding out the arm of the hoodie, "or wool. Stuff like that. Food and paper and small bits of plastic seem to go through okay. My shoes are mostly leather, so they work. If I wear something with too much metal or polyester, it just gets left behind."

Tabitha's eyes got wide. "Like the buckshot! That's why it didn't show up in your wounds."

He nodded. "So it wouldn't do any good to make me some kind of spook assassin. I can't take a gun with me, or a camera, nothing mechanical. I wouldn't if I could."

"But, your watch..." she pointed out. He held out his wrist and looked at it.

"Yeah," he agreed, holding it out for inspection. "It's a machine, I know. The only thing I can think of is I was wearing it the first time it happened. Same thing for the fillings in my teeth. I had to go to a watch maker to have an alarm put in."

Something caught her attention. "Why an alarm?"

He held out the face of the watch. "Twelve mintues. That's how long I have to wait between each time I wink out." He lowered his arm. "I don't know why it's twelve minutes. If I try to fold out before that, nothing happens. That's why I need a watch."

"That's so weird."

He shrugged again. "I know. They're not my rules." They came to a trash can, where he threw away the wrapper and empty water bottle.

She stared at him. "You really are a Boy Scout," she admitted.

"You say that like it's a bad thing," he replied.

"No," she said, "I mean... the file Interpol gave me. With pictures of you at disasters. It looked like you caused them, but that's not right. You teleport to places where there's problems: to help out."

He nodded his head. "Sometimes," he said, "one extra person on the scene really can make a difference." He looked nervously over his shoulder as a car's headlights went by.

"It's okay," she reassured him. "We're alone."

"Are we?" He looked at his watch. "Almost time. So, what happens now? Are you gonna turn me in? I didn't ask if you were wearing a wire. Are there spooks in a van somewhere listening to all this? Am I being tracked by some Predator drone?"

Tabitha pursed her lips. "I'm not turning you in." She shook her head. "Nobody would believe me," she said finally. "I kind of blew my credibility with you already, making you out to be some kind of international terrorist."

Bailey put his hands into his pockets. "There's enough of them already," he said. "Like that Gancho guy."

"What?" She asked, looking closely at him. "What did you say?"

"When I got shot, the main bad guy, the leader of the gunmen who shot down that family," he said. "The others called him Gancho, El Gancho. He was mad about something called Shenzhen..." He turned, and saw the look in her face. Her eyes were wide, her mouth slightly open, and she seemed to be thinking hard about something.

"You know that name," he realized. "It means something to you."

She looked at him, then turned away suddenly. "I really can't say—"

"Hey, I just told you all about me. Who is he?" Bailey pursued. "El Gancho. Where is he from?"

Tabitha's mind was spinning. "I—I took an oath when I joined the CIA," she explained. "Thereare things I can't talk about."

Bailey stopped. His eyes narrowed. "Is he one of your guys?" he asked.

"What?" Tabitha gasped. "Good God, no!" She saw he was grimacing with pain, holding his side again. "Where did you get shot?"

Bailey pointed to his side. "Here. Right here," he said, like it was a silly question.

She shook her head. "No, no, the place! Where were you when you got shot?"

"Columbia, Puerto Bolivar," he said, straightening up.

She blinked in confusion. "Of all places in the world, why there?"

He pointed off into the distance. "I got curious. I saw the name on those papers in your front seat. I looked up pictures of the place on the Internet."

Tabitha slapped herself on the forehead. The State Department briefs; they were in her car when she dropped off his boots.

He drew a breath and looked up. "So who is that guy? An informed source? A protected witness? What?"

"A killer—a very dangerous man!" Tabitha admitted. "This is not somebody you want to be on the same planet with, okay?"

Bailey frowned. "We're already on the same planet," he said.

"Look—there's stuff I can't talk about, because it's my job, but... there's plenty of stuff online, if you know where to look."

Bailey stepped closer, intrigued. "Such as?"

Unconsciously, she looked over her shoulder, then leaned closer in confidence. "Last Summer, July, I think... a newspaper in Italy called *Veritas Moderna* ran an article about El Gancho... I think they have an online archive—" She stopped herself, and turned to face him. "Why do you want to know where to find him? He tried to kill you."

"That guy and his goons killed a whole family," Bailey said. "Maybe I can't stop him, maybe I can't stop any of them, but I can recon his operation. I can cause him some trouble, slow him down, maybe make him mess up so that you guys can stop him."

"Columbia is where he'd be based," she said, stopping herself. She sighed deeply. "This is all classified information. I have security clearance. I took an oath. I should not be talking to you about this!"

His face softened. He stood up straight. "You're right, you shouldn't... and you can't be talking to me, here in Washington D.C.," he said, looking at his watch, "because I'm back home in Pennsylvania." He looked up, his eyes focused over her shoulder. That was when she heard the police siren. She turned at the sound, and saw a DC police car, siren blaring, lights flashing, zoom down a side street.

"Thanks for the watch," he said softly. She could feel his breath on her neck.

Tabitha turned to face him—and found herself completely alone. She whirled around, but there was no one at all in sight. Far off, a car alarm chirped. The breeze had picked up. An army helicopter soared over the Potomac. She ran a hand across her face, and realized her hands were shaking.

"I need a drink..." she decided.

THE SPOOK

CHAPTER 16 – LATE FRIDAY, PORTLAND

Down the hall from the Henry Failing Art and Music Library and around the corner from the drinking fountain was a small research room. Lined with bookshelves, they loomed over a table with two computers. Most of the library's computers were on the first floor, in a line within sight of the main desk, but for the purposes of more private research two were connected in an upstairs office. The lack of internal security cameras was a plus. For people who had never been there before, the research room was difficult to find in the huge library. However, Bailey had been there many times.

The room was just as he remembered it, except for a picture on the wall: a poster of a frog reading a book. He correctly guessed the room would be empty that time on a Friday evening. Sitting at one terminal, he was able to log into the system with a generic username English students had been using for years. Bailey had stumbled across the codes when he found some notebooks left behind on a library table. Anyone doing an audit of the user logs that evening would see no red flags. Still, he took precautions.

The Internet browser came up. Bailey did a search for *Veritas Moderna*, Italy. He found the newspaper's website right away, but translating it into English was tricky. He managed to browse to a mirror site that let him search by subject. He typed in "El Gancho" and hit Enter.

The article was from May of that year. It was not in the news, as he might have thought, but in the celebrity section. The story was about a big party thrown by an Italian movie director:

"...Also on hand was wealthy Columbian businessman Valentin 'the Sailor' Bravo, who shrugged off questions that he was associated with Antonio 'El Gancho' Lopez, head of the deadly *Depredador* drug army. Although he admitted he knew Lopez as a young man, Bravo said those rowdy days are behind him ..."

THE SPOOK

Bailey re-read the passage. That was it? He wondered if there were any photos. The website was hard to navigate. He kept scrolling over to finish sentences. The timer on his watch went off. He kept surfing through websites looking for any images. As he searched for photos, he scrolled back over the party story again... and froze. He read it again, and ended up staring at the words "the Sailor."

Sailor... mariner... El Marinero! Bailey thought. That was the name El Gancho said in the junkyard. He needed to know more. Out of habit, he hid his research with a series of apparently random link searches: Valentine's Day, hearts, holidays throughout the world, decorating houses, expensive Latin American mansions, and finally a link to San Cordero, palatial home of rich businessman Valentin Bravo. An image search brought pictures from a South American magazine. Once he knew the location, he started searching for links to the nearest town, which turned out to be El Penol. Columbia had departments instead of states, and El Penol was in the eastern sub region of the Antioquia Department. He was about to do another search when he looked up and saw a young woman poking her head into the research room.

"Sir? The library will be closing in fifteen minutes."

"Just finishing up," Bailey smiled, logging off the computer.

He took his time leaving, walking down the impressive ninety-two-step staircase to the main lobby. Outside, exterior lights lit up the walls of the Georgian style building. The air was chilly. Streetlights were starting to come on. Portland was pretty that time of year. Bailey walked down the street, turned into a darkened alleyway...

...and was back home. He was in his bathroom again. In the medicine cabinet, he found a bottle of ibuprofen. He swallowed a couple of pills with a handful of water from the faucet. He pulled the grey t-shirt over his head to expose his torso. The bandages on his side were intact, with no bleeding. That was a good sign. He figured he would be completely healed in a couple of days.

He kicked off his shoes on his way to the living room. Out of habit, he turned on the TV news channel. Bailey figured he should eat something, like maybe some soup, but decided he needed a nap first. He muted the sound on the TV, taking it easy as he laid down. Tearing any sutures at this point would be a bad idea. His eyes fluttered with sleep as images flickered on the TV. It had been a long couple of days. He thought about his online research, the heartless junkyard murder, and what his next steps would be.

First, he thought as he drifted off to sleep, he needed to get a new shirt...

THE SPOOK

CHAPTER 17 – FRIDAY EVENING

It was not the most luxurious hotel in the city, nor the most popular, but it had the caveat of multiple entrances and exits, impossible to completely cover, but perfect for discreet rendezvous. The general sipped his whiskey and gazed out the large windows at the city below. Two armed guards stood in the corners, as did two thick-set men in suits, equally armed. But there would be no gunfire that day, the general had promised. His guest had paid handsomely for an audience and he intended to keep his word. For the moment.

A knock came to the door. After a nod from the general, one of the suited gentlemen turned to open it. The general sat down in one of the chairs, making himself comfortable. This encounter should, at least, be entertaining.

He watched as a man with silver hair entered the room. He wore an expensive suit, and wore gold rings on his fingers. His face was chiseled from a hundred back-alley fights, his attitude hardened by years of cruelty. "General Gomez," he greeted.

The general nodded in response. "Good afternoon, Senor Lopez, or should I say El Gancho. Please, sit down."

Gancho sat as his host poured him a drink. "You are looking well, general."

"Thank you, senor," the general said, sliding the glass over. "The war against drugs has been very good to me ... thanks to you."

"I should think so," Gancho admitted. "The country has profited from your grand leadership. And thanks to my inside information, your forces have made many successful raids, and killed many bad men."

"Bad men who, coincidentally, happened to be competitors of your employer, El Marinaro," the general replied, taking a sip. "That has worked out well for all parties."

Gancho shook his head. "Not all, senor general."

Gomez raised an eyebrow. "Oh?"

"True, our collaboration has profited you and the illustrious

El Marinaro, but I am afraid I personally remain... undercompensated for my efforts."

The general put his glass down on the table. "I told you when we began this association my discretionary funds were limited..."

"No, no, general," Gancho interjected, holding up a hand, "it is not my association with you that has left me unhappy, but rather that of my employer, our mutual associate El Marinaro."

"I am sorry to hear that, amigo," the general said. "A loyal worker such as you deserves to be suitably compensated. How do you propose to change this situation?"

"By the elimination of the cause," El Gancho said simply. "El Marinaro remains the last of the grand drug lords of Columbia. It would be quite a feather in your hat to be the one to take him down, would it not?"

The general considered Gancho's words. "You make a provocative point. But a man such as Valentin Bravo can still control loyalty and power even from within a prison cell."

Gancho took a sip of whiskey. "That is why he must die," he said simply. "He and his cancerous offspring. The slate must be wiped clean."

"And what would happen to his organization, the drug business, his wealth and properties?" the general asked. "Who would step in to take control?"

Gancho smiled, his eyes sparkling with mirth. "Someone... appropriate, no doubt. I can arrange for guards to be indisposed, the estate vulnerable. How soon can your men be prepared to move?"

The general pursed his lips. "For an operation this size, two days. I would want to commit all available forces."

"I would expect your usual efficiency in these affairs. And no matter what happens, El Marinaro dies," Gancho emphasized. He downed his shot of whiskey and stood. "I will make preparations and expect your call on... Saturday, is it?"

"Quite so," the general said, standing. "But this operation still requires a semblance of the law. Under what pretext will we be launching this raid?"

"Drugs, of course," Gancho said. "Exotic drugs, narcotics, no doubt. All the way from China. There is nothing else it could be."

THE SPOOK

CHAPTER 18 – SATURDAY MORNING

Tabitha was jolted from sleep by her cellphone buzzing on the nightstand. Now what? She thought as she picked it up. This must be my week for early-morning phone calls. The display said it was a call from Weaver.

"Yes, sir?" she answered.

"Meeting in Conference Room B, 7 AM," replied Weaver. "There've been some new developments I want you to sit in on."

"Room B, seven AM," Tabitha repeated, looking at her bedside clock: 5:22. "I'll be there, sir." Weaver hung up without saying goodbye. Turning on the bedside light, Tabitha wondered what was going on. She'd never been called in on a weekend before. There was no point in going back to bed. She showered, dressed and picked up a breakfast sandwich on the way to CIA headquarters.

She could smell the coffee as soon as she got off the elevator. When she arrived at the conference room, she was surprised to see others got the call as well. A group was clustered around a coffee tray set up by the cafeteria. At least she was not the only one trying to wake up.

She recognized Tidwell, from the Far East Office, who was checking his cellphone, and Hendrix, from European intelligence. Bolton from forensic accounting was setting up her laptop. Pilsbury from the State Department was chatting with an officer in a naval uniform. Chandra Parks from the South America bureau came in as Tabitha poured herself a cup. Pretty eclectic group, she thought.

Tabitha sipped her coffee. "Morning, everybody," she said, trying to be cheerful. "Anybody know what's going on?"

Weaver entered the room and banged his knuckles loudly on the door. "Okay, everyone, please take a seat. We have a situation that needs to be addressed immediately. Seats, please."

As Tabitha took a seat at the long table, she spotted Hank Gannon entering with a laptop and some other equipment. He started setting up in a far corner. "I'm sure everyone knows each other. Let me explain. The situation in question involves the Chinese research facility that was destroyed earlier this week, along with the murder of a dozen scientists. I'll now turn things over to Agent Hendrix."

Hendrix stood up, his hair frizzed in back from some static electricity. "Thank you for coming in this morning. The research facility that was destroyed this past Tuesday was working on a project called *Shenzhen Wu*, possibly a never-before seen biological terrorist weapon."

There was a subdued reaction throughout the room. "What is it?"

"Something that can destroy a whole culture," Hendrix explained. "It took a while for our operatives in China to decode the notes left behind at the facility, and longer for the intel to get to us. Shenzhen is the Chinese city directly adjacent to Hong Kong. That's what threw us. We thought there might be a terrorist event planned for Hong Kong. But it's bigger than that. Shenzhen has another meaning. Shen zhen literally means 'true god,' the force of God at work in our everyday lives. And nothing is more true about the force of God than the act of reproduction. Hana?"

Tabitha recognized Hana Jeong, one of the civilian experts employed by the CIA. "Two years ago," the woman said, standing up, "we caught wind of a project called *Shenzhen Lar*, very secret. As you know, China has had a one-child policy for decades. Every couple is allowed one child, no more. This has put added pressure on finding alternate forms of contraception."

"Is this what all this is about?" Parks asked. "Some super condom or something?" A couple of the men in the room snickered.

"A very expensive one," Hendrix interjected. The tone of his voice reminded everyone of the seriousness at hand. "Contraception is what *Shenzhen Lar* was all about. 'Lar' is the Chinese word for two. *Shenzhen Lar* was phase two of the project. *Shenzhen Wu* represents phase five, a much more advanced state."

"State of what?" Parks insisted. "What was the project about?"

"Contraception," Hendrix said. "Specifically, an aerosol

contraceptive. The scientists in Gansu were working on a spray, a gas, that would make a woman incapable of conceiving a baby. Whoever destroyed the facility and killed those scientists also made off with all the aerosol they had produced."

Tabitha leaned forward, suddenly interested.

"How does the stuff work?" Tidwell asked.

"According to the prospectus," Hendrix said, "it would be like taking a squirt of breath freshener. From what I understand, the inhaled gas enters the bloodstream and starts a chemical chain reaction which prevents conception. One little spritz, the proper dosage, and a woman would be incapable of becoming pregnant for thirty-six hours."

"How far along had they proceeded in their research?" asked one of the men in the back.

"They finished it," said Jeong. "It worked. The Chinese scientists perfected a safe, aerosol contraceptive. The problem was, the cost was astronomical. A year's worth of *Shinzhen Lar* would have cost a fortune, far beyond even the wants of the wealthiest customers. The Chinese determined it was not profitable in the long run. Funding was cut and the project was scrapped."

"Officially scrapped," Hendrix clarified. "Somehow, the project kept going, until they perfected the advanced version, *Shinzhen Wu*. Somehow, the research facility acquired funding to continue."

Weaver stepped in. "That's where your team comes in, Callie." He pointed to Callie Bolton, head of forensic accounting. "I need your team to scan the records we recovered from China. Find out who was bankrolling this operation."

Bolton nodded, and made some notes on a pad of paper.

Tidwell was shaking his head. "I don't understand how this concerns national security. Why the CIA would be involved."

Tabitha spoke up. "Why would terrorists care about a contraceptive?" she asked.

"Yeah," echoed Pilsbury, who was sitting next to her. "Can it be combined with something else to make something toxic, or explosive? Something poisonous?"

"We don't know how volatile it is under pressure. All we know from the recovered documents," Jeong said, "is that it must stay under 200° Fahrenheit. Otherwise, it should be safe for transport."

"So," said Tidwell, "what makes it so dangerous?"

"If Shenzhen two worked," Bolton asked, "was Shenzhen five a cheaper version?"

Hendrix shook his head. "I'm getting to that. Under the pretext of making it cheaper, they made the drug stronger, more potent. At the proper dosage, it still did the job it was designed for. But according to the files recovered from the scene, anything over the proper dosage... has the capacity to render a woman sterile. The effect is immediate and permanent. There's also a possibility the gas can make men sterile as well."

A collective murmur rose from the room. Weaver knocked his knuckles on the top of the table. "That's what makes this a biological weapon, people. A terror weapon. At sufficient quantities, a terrorist could sterilize an entire population of people. A city full of people. Right?"

Hendrix nodded his head. "A city at least."

"Sufficient quantities? How much quantity are we talking about?"

"It's like what Paracelsus said, back in the German Renaissance," Hendrix explained. "Everything's a poison and everything has poison in it. A glass of water is fine but an ocean will drown you, like that. It's the dosage that makes it dangerous."

"The proper dosage," Jeong said, looking at her tablet, "the recommended dosage, is two nanoliters, or two one-billionths of a liter." The glazed stares around the room prompted her to clarify. "Okay, let me put it this way. One microliter is equal to one one-millionth of a liter. It would be the amount of one cubic millimeter, a cube the size of the edge of a dime. Two nanoliters would be a pair of cubes a thousand times smaller than a microliter."

"So," said Bolton slowly, "you're saying one liter would be enough to work on a billion people?"

"Half a billion," said Jeong. "Two cubes, remember? Exposure to anything more than that per person would cause sterilization."

"Oh, my God," breathed Tabitha. "Half a billion people?"

"If that's what a liter would do," said the navy major, speaking for the first time, "how much did the terrorists steal from the China facility?"

Jeong did not have to look at her notes. "Three hundred liters," she said grimly. "About eighty gallons."

Several people gasped. "That much could sterilize the western hemisphere," Tidwell calculated.

"How," said Parks, clearing her throat, "how is it being transported?"

"Documents recovered from the China facility indicate we're looking for a cylinder, about six feet long and three feet in diameter."

The man behind Tabitha shifted in his seat. She turned to see it was Agent Conrad. "It's the size of a refrigerator," he muttered. She had not noticed when he came into the room.

Weaver rapped his knuckles on a table to get everyone's attention. "Here's the deal, people. The Chinese government is embarrassed this happened under their noses, so we'll get no cooperation from them. We're going by what we know according to satellite images and internet chatter. And it's not good. That stuff is out there and we need to find it. Understood?"

"So where is this stuff now?" Tidwell asked.

Hendrix pointed to a world map on the wall. "After the original facility was destroyed, we believe the *Shenzhen Wu* was taken overland to Kazakhstan, where it was airlifted to Sweden. Our contacts in our Swedish embassy say it was supposed to have been put on a freighter called the Wushu Senator, bound for the Middle East."

"What do you mean, supposed to?" Bolton asked.

"For some reason, it was diverted from the freighter and loaded onto a plane. Either the thieves themselves got hijacked, or the freighter may have been a diversion all along to confuse hijackers. The stuff cost millions to produce and could be worth billions in the long run."

"So, who's in control?" Weaver said. "Who has it? Who paid for the development, and who are their customers?"

"Follow the money," Pilsbury nodded.

"If it's that expensive," said Tidwell, "there would be a limited number of clients for the product. There's only so many individuals or terrorist groups that could afford such a weapon. That should narrow our focus a little."

Tabitha's eyes got wide and she gasped to herself as she realized she'd heard the word "Shenzhen" before—from Bailey!

They'd want to know her source. What could she say? Weaver noticed her reaction. "Something to add, Tabitha?"

"Well," she said, clearing her throat, "it ...wouldn't be simply terrorists after this stuff. We should also look at third parties, people who are only in it for the profit. People who would want it to sell to terrorists. Intermediaries, dealers, like that."

Weaver nodded. "Good thinking. This could be corporate espionage. Okay, here's what I want us to do..."

Assignments went out, and everyone focused on their various tasks... except Tabitha, who couldn't stop thinking about what Bailey said. Had he found the *Shenzhen Wu*? In Columbia, of all places? What else did he know? Where was he now? If she told Weaver what she knew, she would be exposing both her and Bailey, but the threat of the S-5 overrode every other consideration. No matter what, Tabitha decided, she had to figure out a way to contact Bailey, and soon.

CHAPTER 19 – SATURDAY MORNING

When Bailey woke, he was still on the couch. He'd slept for almost ten hours. He sat up slowly, his left side stiff and sore. Gingerly, he peeled back the bandage. The buckshot wounds had healed nicely, but were still tender. He replaced the bandage and got up to fix himself some breakfast.

After a bite to eat and a dash through the shower, Bailey sat down at his computer. He needed to find this Valentin Bravo character, somewhere near El Penol, Columbia. A search for images immediately brought up the Rock of Guatapéa, a gigantic rock outside of town. A broader search found El Penol was on the southwest corner of Embalse Del Penol, a lake formed when the country put in a hydroelectric dam. Pablo Escobar had a home nearby. The lake created dozens of islands, most of which were home to Medillin's elite. San Cordero was not on one of them, but on the eastern bank of the Embalse Del Penol, deep inside Bravo's private little bay.

Bailey found his other black BDU shirt in his closet and pulled on his leather, fingerless gloves. Browsing on the Internet, he looked at satellite photos and found two roads leading into the San Cordero estate. He noticed the photos were two years old, so that meant everything could be different. He searched for pictures of the town and found a couple of markets on side streets that were easy to remember. One market had a sign with a smiling monkey high over the front door. He thought of the monkey...

...and was immediately drenched with water. It was raining in El Penol, the storm coming down in buckets. Bailey reminded himself to check the weather reports next time. He was alone on the wet street, rainwater pouring down the gutters in front of the market. The monkey sign smiled down at him. He set the timer on his watch. There was an icy chill in the air. Bailey had also forgotten to note what elevation the town was at.

Well, now what? He asked himself. He could not just thumb

a ride to a drug empire. Bailey shivered against the chill. He had to set priorities. The first thing was to get inside somewhere, out of the weather.

He walked down the narrow sidewalk. Rain came down evenly, with no wind to knock it about. Ahead, the concrete sidewalks were cracked, and the street pockmarked with holes. Rain slipped straight down between the narrow buildings and ran freely down along the curb. It soaked his hair and drenched his clothes. He thought he heard music.

The faded sign in front of the short brick building read Cantina. Rusty beer signs were tacked around the thick front door. Peeling paint along the sides framed years of political posters, torn and faded, that had been plastered along the wall. Bailey's hand felt the outside of his pocket, and was glad he brought some cash along.

The locals took little notice of the gringo as he came into the cantina. Another lost tourist, they thought. The bartender, a large, sweaty man in a dingy t-shirt, nodded to him as he sat down on a bar stool. Bailey pointed to a bottle of a local, cheap beer, so the bartender brought him one. He held up three one-dollar bills, and raised his eyebrows in question. The bartender, no doubt used to ignorant gringos, nodded and took the cash. He did not bring back any change.

Bailey took a sip from the bottle of beer. It was just one big room, the bar stretched almost the entire length. Four round tables lined the opposite wall. None of the chairs matched.

Bailey had no plan, no agenda. He was about to leave when he noticed a pair of the locals way in the back, sitting far from the front door. One of them seemed... familiar, somehow. That seemed unlikely. He had never been to Colombia before, and the only other time he had met up with Colombian thugs had been when he got shot in Puerto Bolivar. And one of the shooters was sitting not thirty feet from him! Not the one that shot him. It was the friend of the man with the shotgun, the one with the flashlight. He wore a new shirt, and had shiny new shoes. Being a hired killer must pay well. Several empty beer bottles sat in front of him on the table. The other man at the table was very drunk, and paid him little attention as he talked.

The buzzer on Bailey's watch went off. He turned it off as he rose from the barstool. If that short man was here, the other killers may be nearby, too. Bailey did not stop. He walked to the front door and slipped out into the dark, rainy street.

Estiban turned to order another beer when he first noticed the man in the black shirt. Some dumb gringo, he thought at first. Not worth thinking about. No good for anything. Like he had been saying all evening, the gringos were too dumb to take care of themselves, to provide for their families—But just then, a chill went down Estiban's spine. That face. He had seen that gringo somewhere before.

Then, he remembered. The bartender stared as Estiban's eyes got wide with terror. Even his drunk friend woke up enough to notice the color had drained out of Estiban's face. He swung his hand around, grabbing at the table to steady himself, loudly knocking beer bottles against each other. He pulled himself to his feet and ran to the front door.

"Hey!" cried the bartender. "Are you going pay for all that?"

Estiban threw the heavy front door open and burst out onto the street. Rain slapped him in the face, and he squinted at the water in his eyes. Only a lone streetlight illuminated the corner where the cantina sat. Several old cars sat parked along the street, but other than that, the street was empty. There was no one in sight anywhere. He listened for footsteps, but only heard car engines, radio music, a distant bell, and the constant patter of the rain. The gringo had disappeared. The witch, he meant! The witch had been swallowed back into the earth! He had followed them to wreak vengeance on the living! Estiban was shaking with fear as he walked back into the cantina.

"What is your problem?" the bartender asked. "Did you want another beer?"

"Yes. No!" Estiban said suddenly. "Tequila! And leave the bottle!"

Minutes later a large car pulled up to the cantina. The car honked once, then again. After a minute, a tall man got out of the car and entered the cantina. Estiban sat in a chair, his back against the wall, the bottle of tequila on the table within reach. A .45 automatic pistol was also close by, tucked into the waistband of his trousers.

THE SPOOK

The pony-tailed man stormed into the cantina, not at all pleased. Benito had places to go, and did not have time to waste. He was visibly surprised when he saw his friend, slumped deep into his chair, a bottle of tequila nearby.

"What are you doing?" cried Benito. "Are you stupid or something?"

"He was here, Benito," said Estiban, his voice almost a whisper, his eyes darting up and down the length of the bar. "He was here, in the bar."

"Who?" Benito asked, suddenly interested. "Who was here?"

Estiban leaned closer in confidence. "The witch. The witch from the docks!"

Benito stared at his friend for a moment. In one swift movement, he drew his arm back and slapped the bottle off the table. Tequila went spilling everywhere.

"You idiot!" cried Benito. "Why do I keep you around? You and your stupid superstitious nonsense!" Benito pushed the other man to the floor and kicked at Estiban's chest. Estiban curled up in a fetal position to protect himself.

"No, no, Benito! I tell you the truth!" cried Estiban. Tears were rolling down his round cheeks. "He was here!"

Benito grunted, and looked back at the bartender. "Was anyone here? A gringo?"

"Si," said the bartender. "He drank a beer and left." The bartender shrugged his shoulders. "All gringos look alike to me."

"Him too, obviously!" Benito said, pointing at Estiban. "Get up! I do not have time for children's fairy tales! Get up and get your miserable, drunken ass in the car right now!"

"All right! All right!" pleaded Estiban. "I will get up!" The shorter man slowly rose to his feet.

"Idiot!" Benito turned on his heels, his pony tail whipping across his back, as he stormed towards the front door, the humbled Estiban following close behind. Outside, Benito waited for Estiban to open the door of the car. When Estiban started to crawl inside, Benito gave him one last boot to the backside before following him inside.

As the car pulled away from the cantina, no one bothered to

106

look up the street. Through the rain, two blocks away, framed by the plain buildings, was an old Christian church. Built in the 1920's, it had weathered storms, earthquakes and revolutions, its steeple standing tall the whole time. The rain had turned into a steady drizzle, like a heavy, dripping fog.

Except for hitting his head on the bell in the steeple, Bailey had managed to wink up there with no incident. It was the highest place he could see from the front of the cantina. From the vantage point, he waited, hidden back inside the bell tower. He weathered the storm until the car arrived. He knew the moment the tall man emerged from the back of the vehicle that it was the one that had shot him. The pony tail was unmistakable, even from that distance. Bailey waited, and soon he returned with his friend, now obviously stumbling. The brake lights flashed, and the car pulled away from the curb. He watched the tail lights as they bounced down the street and disappeared around a corner.

Bailey stood, careful to not bump the large iron bell again, and moved to another side of the tower. There had to be a way to follow it, he decided. Bailey checked his watch. He had just popped to the bell tower. He stared into the drizzling rain, looking for options. The streets below were empty, except parked next to a telephone pole on the opposite side of the church there was an old pickup. Bailey dashed for the stairs and hurried to the ground level.

Stepping out of the church and back into the rain was like walking into a shower. Bailey shook his head and rushed across the street to the pickup. It was an older model, heavily dented with a cracked windshield. But since it was parked on the street, it apparently still worked. He reached for the door handle—

... But then he stopped himself. He couldn't just take it, could he? That would be stealing. He looked down the street where the killer's car went, then back at the pickup, the conflict twisting inside him. *Maybe I could just borrow it*, he thought. *Borrow it for a while, just until I see where the truck's going, then bring it right back.*

The truck bed was full of garbage: wet, soggy boxes, empty bottles, a plastic sack full of crushed beer cans. Whoever owned the truck probably took the keys with him. Couldn't hurt to look, he thought, running a hand across his face. He could leave a note under the windshield wiper. Apologize for borrowing it. Fill it with gas before bringing it back. Bailey casually looked around for witnesses, then opened the driver's door of the pickup.

The foot came at him out of nowhere. It kicked at him from the interior of the pickup, barely missing his chin. It was an elderly Latino man, his hair streaked with silver. He had been lying across the bench seat of the pickup, as if taking a nap. He had grabbed the steering wheel and was pulling himself up to a sitting position.

"Ladron!" the man cried. "Thief!"

"No, wait," Bailey said, holding up his gloved hands. "I was just gonna borrow it—"

The man hopped out of the pickup, swinging a flashlight like a club. "Ladron! Ladron!"

"Wait!" Bailey said, wishing again that he spoke Spanish. The man, middle-aged with a scraggly grey beard, reared back for another swing with his flashlight. Bailey could smell alcohol on his breath and clothes. Bailey dodged out of the way of the strike, which threw the man off-balance. He slipped and fell to the wet asphalt ground.

Bailey actually started to help the man back up when he spotted something shiny inside the cab of the pickup. It was a ring of keys, dangling from the ignition. He took one more look at the man on the ground, decided the old man was not hurt, and jumped into the pickup. He started the engine and had it in gear before the old man got back to his feet.

"I'll bring it back, I promise!" Bailey yelled out the open window as he stomped on the gas. The pickup lurched forward, tail pipe coughing, as Bailey turned it down the rainy street. He could hear the old man yelling at him from far behind. *Poor guy*, Bailey thought. *Probably just trying to get by, and somebody up and takes his truck.* He decided he would make it up to the man somehow.

He turned the corner where he last saw the car and floored the gas pedal, pushing the pickup as fast as it could go. Which was not much. He was soon outside of town. Empty paper cups skittered across the dashboard as he made a sharp curve. Three miles down the road he came to a crossroads. There were no other vehicles in sight, much

TIM FRAYSER

less the car.

Bailey looked up and down the dark two-lane, and almost gave up when he spotted something rolling around off to the right, beside the road. It was an insulated coffee cup, empty and recently discarded. Bailey smiled. He turned the pickup to the right and zoomed down the road. Most of the roads in Colombia were two-lane; no interstate highways here, not even the Pan-American Highway, the almost-complete series of roads from Alaska to Tierra Del Fuego.

The old pickup's windshield wipers streaked across the glass. It was hard to see up ahead. To his right, the road branched off to a large pair of gates. An armed sentry stood in a guard house. Bailey kept driving. Did the car pull in there? He slowed down, and noticed fresh mud tracks leading through the gate. He kept going down the narrow, tree-lined road.

He could see movement through the trees off to his right. He pulled off the road, avoiding the water-filled ditch and shut off the engine. He could feel the pickup slightly lurch to the side. Bailey got out and quietly closed the door. A quick inspection showed the trucks tires had sunk into the mud of the ditch. Bailey sighed. He estimated the pickup could free itself form the mud but it would take some effort. In the meantime, he had bad guys to find. He made his way down the road and climbed over a short wire fence.

Rain continued to patter all around him. The storm had turned day into night. Water soaked into his boots and under his gloves. He angled away from the road deeper into the woods. A clearing appeared. He saw other vehicles parked nearby.

Inching his way through the dark, wet jungle, Bailey worked his way around to where he could see what was going on. The rain muffled the sound of rustling leaves underfoot as he made his way through the trees. The clearing was several acres wide. He could see two vehicles already there. A half dozen figures were walking around. Beneath the bough of a large tree, two figures huddled near an old oil barrel. Flames flickered near the rim. Off to the left was the killer's car, parked next to a big flatbed truck. A tarp covered a large object on the back.

He'd found them. He had to get closer. He checked his watch. He could wink over, but he had to see what was under that tarp. He could get out in a hurry if he had to.

109

THE SPOOK

Bailey began working his way clockwise around the clearing. It was slow going, but the trees and bushes provided him with plenty of cover. The bad guys must have been very confident, he decided, since they had not posted any sentries around their perimeter.

When he got to the far side of the clearing, Bailey had to go deeper into the woods to keep his cover. He crawled closer. Flashlight beams pierced the night. Several of the shadowy figures had gathered at the back of the trailer. "We should be on our way," one voice said.

They're speaking English? Bailey wondered.

"No rush, senor," said another, deeper voice from near the burn barrel. "Come, have a drink!" The group moved away from the trailer, leaving the container doors open. Bailey found himself on the far side of the trailer from the burn barrel, where everyone seemed to be headed. He had the cover of the shadows.

The truck was parked parallel to a long building. There was no one within sight. He took a chance and rushed forward from the brushes, keeping low, hoping his footsteps on the muddy ground were not too loud. Bailey inched along the wall and peeked through one of the windows. He could see rows of bunk beds, clothes hanging on a line, a radio on a shelf: living quarters. This must be where the goons are billeted, he thought. Nobody seemed to be inside. He looked around for guards, sentries, anyone keeping an eye on things.

He made it to the trailer. Huddling behind the big wheels of the rear axle, he listened for any alarms. All the sounds were coming from the burn barrel, where a bottle was apparently being passed around. The tree offered minimal protection from the rain. So far, so good, he thought. He stood and quickly moved to the far side of the trailer, where he boosted himself up.

Peeking under the tarp, he found a large cylinder. There were letters painted on the side; Chinese or Japanese, Bailey guessed. The metal felt cold to the touch. What was it? Nitro glycerine? Cooking oil? He had no way of knowing. It seemed funny to have half a dozen gunmen protecting a container of shaving cream, Bailey thought. Whatever it was, it was important to them... which suddenly made it important for Bailey to mess with.

Bailey looked around. He had no weapons, no explosives, no way to even call for help. If it was nitro, he thought, it might not be a good idea to just push it off the truck bed. He felt around the sides of the container, looking for something, anything. What he found was a thin metal spike, probably used to secure the locks. It was sharp at one end. That gave him an idea.

He quickly hopped down and slipped to the dark side of the trailer. Kneeling behind the rear axle of the trailer, he shoved the spike into the tire, puncturing it. The tire made a hissing sound when he withdrew the spike. He froze, listening for footsteps. All was silent. The interior tire was harder to get to. He had to crawl under the trailer, partially exposing himself, but he managed to puncture it and get back into the shadows without detection.

The tires were already halfway flat when Bailey worked his way to the front of the trailer. He was on the passenger side of the big rig. Bailey went to work puncturing all the tires on that side of the truck. He had just pulled the spike out of the truck's right front tire when a chill went down his neck. He had the distinct feeling he was being watched.

Bailey slowly looked over his right shoulder. There was a silhouette of a man standing about four paces away, just past the right front corner of the truck.

"¿qué usted está haciendo?" the man said.

Bailey turned a little more, and the man was able to see his whole face. He started to say something, then stood for a moment staring. Bailey recognized him from his shirt. It was the round-faced man from the cantina, one of the men from the junkyard. Bailey spotted the gun in the man's waistband. He measured the distance, and decided he could not make it to the man before he drew his weapon—which he was already doing.

"Witch!" the man shouted. "Demon!" He fired the gun once, striking the cab of the truck just over Bailey's head.

Bailey ducked and crawled as fast as he could on all fours away from the shooter.

"Monster! Demon!" the man shouted as he fired wildly, the bullets whizzing over Bailey's head, loudly bouncing off the container, or striking the ground with wet thumps.

THE SPOOK

Slipping on the wet grass, Bailey turned and crawled under the trailer just behind the truck's rear tires.

Time to go, he decided. Someplace safe, like home, maybe get a nice hot shower—but then, he remembered the pickup. He promised to bring it back. If he blinked out now, the bad guys would find the pickup and just keep it. He could blink straight to the pickup, but the bad guys might catch up to him before he worked it out of the ditch—and before he could blink away again. Groaning in frustration, he climbed out from under the truck and dashed for the trees.

The others around the campfire came running at the sound of the shots, weapons drawn. The gunmen circled the big rig. There were more shouts, and some more shooting, before Benito managed to arrive. He fired his gun in the air to get the other's attention.

"Shut up! Shut up!" he cried. "What is going on here?"

"It was the ghost!" Estiban declared, still waving his gun. "The witch who sinks into the earth! He was here—he followed us from the cantina!"

Benito frowned at Estiban. "What the hell are you babbling?" He froze, staring at the truck.

"He crawled under there!" Estiban insisted, pointing at the truck. "Look! Look for yourself!"

Benito indeed stepped forward slowly. He snatched a flashlight from one of the others and shone it ahead of him. One by one, the light revealed the tires on the truck and trailer, all flat.

"You shot out the tires!" Benito whispered to himself. Then louder: "You stupid idiot, you shot out the tires!"

One of the other gunmen crawled under the truck, flashlight in one hand, pistol in the other. He emerged from behind one of the flat tires. "There is no one under here, senor."

"What?" said Estiban. "No, no, I—I—" he stammered.

Benito frowned. "You're still drunk, aren't you? Give me your gun," he said as he stepped closer, hand outstretched.

"I—I did not mean—" Estiban was saying. He shook his head in confusion. "I saw him!" he insisted again. He let out a heavy breath, and then placed the automatic in Benito's hand.

Benito took the gun and turned towards the nearest light. "I have had enough of you," he muttered. He pulled back the slide and saw that there was still one bullet left in the chamber. Without another word, he turned back towards Estiban, leveled the weapon—

"Benito, look!" cried one of the other gunmen. Benito looked off to his right and saw a dark figure far off in the woods, moving fast. He turned to the others.

"What are you waiting for? Get him!"

Four of the gunmen rushed into the trees. Benito tucked the gun into his waistband as Estiban gasped.

"You—you were going to shoot me!"

"But I didn't," Benito said calmly. "You're welcome."

Bailey rushed through the thick trees, slipping on wet undergrowth and scratching his face on fallen branches. He slipped and fell, his hands sinking into the wet mud. His clothes were soaked and he could feel water sloshing around in his boots when he finally reached the road. It felt good to get solid asphalt under his feet. Bailey could hear shouts behind him deep in the trees. He saw the old pickup a hundred yards down the road and ran as fast as he could.

Gasping for breath, he made it to the pickup and jumped behind the wheel. The engine turned over first try. His clothes were caked with mud and leaves. Ahead, he could see men with guns on the road coming for him. He put the pickup in reverse and gunned the engine, wheels spitting mud everywhere. The truck shuddered as it pulled itself free of the mud and rushed backwards, bouncing back onto the asphalt road.

Gunshots rang out. Something hit one of the side mirrors. Bailey couldn't see out the back window because of all the garbage in the truck bed, but he caught a glimpse of a side road coming up. He angled towards the opening right as a huge white shape appeared to his right. The Tundra came out of nowhere, roaring down the road and smashing into the passenger side of the pickup. The force rocked the older vehicle up on two wheels and slammed Bailey's head against the driver's door. The pickup came down to rest with a jolt. Bailey was rattled; his hands felt like catcher's mitts on the steering wheel. He tried to focus but everything got blurry; he slumped over on the bench seat unconscious.

A man jumped out of the Tundra, a chrome-plated automatic in his hand. He ran to the pickup and pulled open the door. The others converged on the now destroyed pickup. "Who is it, Tony?" Benito cried out.

The man called Tony emerged from inside the cab. "I never saw him before, senor," said the gunman. "He is unconscious, but still alive."

Tony directed two others to pull the driver from the cab. Benito watched their progress. The dazed man wore a black shirt, just like the mysterious man on the docks. *Could Estiban be correct?* Benito wondered. *Was it the same man?* Tony walked over to Benito. "What about the truck? It will not make the journey back to the coast with tires like that."

"Drive it up to the big house as well," Benito said. "Senor Bravo has a garage for his fancy cars. The tires can be repaired there."

The incessant rain began to let up. Tony cocked his head at the stranger. "What about him?"

Benito nodded. "Bring him to the big house as well," he said. "Whoever he is, Senor Bravo will want to see him personally."

CHAPTER 20 – SATURDAY AFTERNOON

Different groups were hard at work tracking down the *Shenzhen Wu*. From her cubicle, Tabitha could see agents from the Far East office, Europe, a couple of officers from the Pentagon, translators, forensic accountants, even men from the DEA. Tabitha was searching Latin American news reports. Weaver entered the room and clapped his hands. Everyone looked up.

"All right, people," he called. "Status report! Where are we on this?"

"The package was definitely in Sweden," said Tidwell. "It was in the port of Norrkoping, but moved to Linkoping Airport. That's where it was put on a cargo plane."

"A plane going where?" Weaver asked.

"It had three stops on its itinerary. London, Lisbon, and Chamasirrahu."

Bolton frowned. "Where the hell is Chama-whatsit?"

"Columbia." Tabitha got an idea, and started typing away at her computer.

"So who's bankrolling this operation?" Weaver asked. "Anybody?"

One of the accountants raised his hand. "We have accounts going to the staff of the Chinese facility from a holding company in Munich. We've traced the funds to three different corporations in three different countries, and they all go to a Swiss account. We're still waiting on info from Switzerland on who owns that account."

"Sir," said Jeong, standing next to one of the translators, "we have additional news about the package itself." That got Weaver's attention.

"The numbers were not completely translated when the lab documents first arrived," she explained. "We have since gone over the calculations with scientists from Georgetown. The gas is much more concentrated than first estimated, maybe more than was originally intended."

"So it could cover a wider area?" Weaver interjected.

"Possibly," said Jeong." But it also means the mixture is highly unstable."

A silence fell over the room. "We need to find this stuff now!"

"Can we get more information on the intel?" asked a man in short sleeves. "Where did these new documents come from?"

Weaver said, "They were delivered by courier to the U.S. Consulate in Almaty, Kazakhstan. They originally came from one of our operatives, a businessman from Syria. We haven't had any additional contact since. I'm afraid I can't be any more specific."

"Was his name Amir Shamoun?" Tabitha asked. Weaver slowly turned, his eyes wide with surprise.

"How—what makes you say that?" Weaver asked.

Tabitha pointed to her computer screen. "News from Columbia," she said simply. "Amir Shamoun, his wife Shea and his son were found murdered in a remote area of Puerto Benito a couple of days ago. It says police are looking for leads. Right now, it doesn't look like a robbery. More like an assassination."

Parks, the Latin America agent, looked up. "Puerto Benito is down the road from Chamasirrahu Airport."

Weaver was about to say something when a man in short sleeves came up behind him. His badge said he was Dean, DEA. "Amir Shamoun? He's dead?"

Weaver looked over his shoulder. "You know him?"

"He's—well, okay, he was one of our confidential informants in Latin America, sending us info on the drug trade. He was currently working for one of the last drug lords in Columbia: Valentin Bravo."

Weaver snapped his fingers. "That's it! That must be who's been bankrolling this operation."

"Wait, why would a drug lord want with a biological weapon?" Agent Dean asked.

"Another investment," said the accountant. "According to the Munich holding company, over two million dollars has been filtered towards the Chinese lab in the last two years. At first glance, it could have looked like a legitimate investment in pharmaceutical research."

Parkes nodded with understanding. "Except this investment was in biological weapons."

Weaver pointed to Dean and the other DEA agents. "Get me everything about this Bravo character. Coordinate with State. We'll need to search all his properties and secure the Shenzhen compound before it's got a chance to be used."

At that, one of the officers in the corner, a major, stepped close to Weaver. His nametag said Polsky. "May we have a word, sir?"

Images from the newspaper story were still on Tabitha's computer screen. She scrolled across the main image and saw stacks of tires in the background, like it was a... junkyard. Her heart jumped a beat when she realized that must have been the shooting where Bailey was hurt. The one where he almost died.

"Man and his family, huh?" Tabitha almost jumped when Agent Reed spoke. She had not realized he was standing right behind her. "Sounds like El Gancho."

That name! "El Gancho?" she asked calmly.

"Hitman for Bravo, *El Marinaro*," Dean explained. "It's the *Depredator* style to kill a man's whole family when he is targeted. Leave no one behind to seek revenge. Gomez had been after him for years."

Tabitha scrolled down, where the newspaper had a portrait of Shamoun's wife. She looked proud, decent, innocent. "Why hasn't Gomez caught him yet? Doesn't he have a whole army unit at his disposal?"

"Gomez's 'troops,' and I use the word lightly, are little more than thugs and mercenaries. They don't investigate, they strike, but only when it makes Gomez look good." Someone waved to Agent Reed and he hurried away.

She wondered where Weaver had gone. Tabitha went to the break room to refresh her coffee. On the way, she passed a small conference room. Weaver and the army major were having a discussion. The door was cracked, and Tabitha could not help but stop to listen.

"If this weapon can do what you say it can do, we should take immediate action."

"Agreed," she heard Weaver say. "Isn't there a carrier strike group in the Caribbean? Could they secure the container?"

"We could have boots on the ground in two hours," Major

Polsky said, "if we choose to take possession."

"What do you mean choose? We can't allow a weapon like this to fall into the hands of a foreign government."

"We need to look at the big picture," Polsky said. "A weapon like this could be a huge deterrent of war for anyone who possesses it."

"Yes, it could, but—"

"But," interrupted Polsky, lowering his voice, "an untested weapon is no deterrent at all."

Tabitha blinked.

Weaver's voice: "Are you saying we should let some terrorist use this gas, let them sterilize an entire population, just to show the world it works?"

"Mutually-assured destruction kept the world safe from nuclear weapons for over forty years," Polsky said. "But without Hiroshima and Nagasaki, no one would have been convinced of its potential."

Weaver was silent for a moment. "We could monitor the weapon, follow it, and then after someone uses it, swoop in and take control."

"Exactly," said Polsky. "Like nuclear weapons, it may be only a matter of time before others discover the same technology—or, in this case, the same chemistry. As a matter of national security, the United States should take the lead with this."

"The terrorists would get the blame, and America would get the credit for stopping the weapon—by keeping it for ourselves." Weaver said, slowly.

"Of course," Polsky added, "the U.S. would never use such a devastating weapon against a foreign power... unless provoked."

Tabitha knocked on the door and pushed it open. "Anybody want any coffee?" she tried to ask cheerfully.

Back at her desk, Tabitha was stunned. They were going to let terrorists use the *Shenzhen Wu*, use it to sterilize an entire population, just to take it for themselves! For *ourselves*, she corrected herself, and immediately felt shame at the whole idea. There had to be options. She needed more information—specifically, information from Bailey. He was on the ground, he heard the bad guys, was indeed almost killed by them. She needed to know what else Bailey knew. Casually, she pulled out her cellphone and sent a text to Bailey: *Call me! As soon as possible!*

THE SPOOK

CHAPTER 21 -- THREE YEARS PAST

A face full of dust blew through the open flap in the tent and hit Bailey right in the eyes. It got up under his helmet and down his collar. He spat out dust as he wiped a hand across his brow.

Afghanistan sucks! he decided as he pulled the flap aside and left the tent. He was cold, he was hungry, and he was overloaded with gear in the middle of Hell. Bailey walked half a dozen steps before he realized there was a rock in his boot. *Lovely,* he thought. His back ached from all the digging he had done the day before: irrigation trenches. A fellow Guardsman grunted as he walked towards the latrine. Bailey grunted back. It was too early in the day for words.

There were twenty soldiers on the short ridge, all from the Pennsylvania National Guard. They were camped with two personnel carriers, one water tanker truck, one Humvee and a dozen Afghan nationals. The Afghans were transporting the water, and they were there to escort the Afghans.

The plan was to transport a thousand gallons of water to a remote mountain village fifty miles north of Kabul. Easy-peasy, the brass told them. Drive up, drop off the water, drive on back. Six hours, tops.

It did not work out that way. The convoy was still in the suburbs of Kabul when they were hit with an IED. The whole road just erupted in front of them like a volcano. The lead vehicle got lucky. The bomb went off early, and just showered the Humvee with dirt, rocks and broken asphalt. Of course, they had to secure the area, check for damage, and make sure nobody was injured. But they had to backtrack and take another route. Bailey had crouched in the personnel carrier, rifle at ready, expecting small arms fire the whole time they were circling around, but none emerged. It was a relief to get out of the city and into the country.

By that time, however, it was early evening, so the convoy set up camp, establish a perimeter, set up checkpoints, and reconnected by satellite hookup with US command back in

THE SPOOK

Kabul.

It was an uneasy but uneventful night on the road. The next day, they found the maps to the village were wrong. Their Afghan companions were little help, getting into arguments with other passing locals every time the convoy stopped for directions. Bailey could not understand the words, but the conversations all seemed pretty lively. Arguments almost broke out several times. The convoy spent yet another night on the road.

And so it went as they made their way into the mountains. When they finally found the village, they discovered there was no tank to dump the water. Someone had told the villagers the generous Americans were just going to leave them the water truck. That would not do. Their Afghan assistants got into more arguments, this time acting as translators between the villagers and the arguing American officers.

The argument went up the line over satellite hookups all the way to the State Department, where someone decided, in the interest of winning hearts and minds, they should abandon dropping off the water and instead dig a well for the village. This was a grand idea, much appreciated by the villagers and considered a happy compromise by State Department officials on the other side of the world... except Bailey's convoy had brought no such well-digging equipment with them. The equipment had to be airlifted in, which meant they needed a place to land, which meant they needed equipment to clear the land for the aircraft to land so that they could get the equipment to dig a well for the village.

Bailey calculated they were currently in the tenth day of their six-hour mission.

"Bailey!" barked a voice up ahead. It was Weems, the sergeant. He stood half a foot shorter than anyone else in the unit, but made up for it with anger. "Bailey, get over here!"

"Sir!" answered Bailey, trotting over to the sergeant. Weems stood on a small rise overlooking a rocky valley. Dead grass bent in the winter breeze. The spot where Weems stood put him above the eye level of everyone else. Bailey suspected he did it on purpose.

"Bailey," the sergeant growled, "I want you to take guard duty first shift tonight."

"Tonight?" Bailey asked. He had hoped for a day of rest.

"Yeah, why?" the sergeant grumbled. "You got a date? Collins tripped and twisted his ankle," Weems explained. "Need you to fill in a day or so."

"First shift," he repeated. "Yes, sir. I'll be there, sir."

"And give first platoon a hand digging that latrine!" Weems dismissed him with a grumpy wave and resumed looking through a pair of binoculars. The air was dry, and the sky was a pale blue, with some feathery clouds off to the north. Bailey headed off to the camp mess to pick up his breakfast.

The unit had made camp about a half mile from the little village. There were no trees, and only a few bushes across the flat plain. A handful of villagers milled about the camp, helping the soldiers and doing menial tasks. The only thing worth guarding in the camp was the helicopter pad, which had been roped off with a four-foot-high fence. It gave the camp its official name: Landing Zone 465.

Bailey walked down the slope to the mess. The "mess" was just a tent where they kept their crates of MRE's. The army was not going to spend time and resources building a decent mess tent for what was officially still a six-hour mission. One of the personnel trucks stayed parked next to it, within easy-loading distance, in the ongoing hope they could pack up quickly if the word came to go back to Kabul soon. Bailey was surprised to find a box of fresh strawberries that had somehow made their way up from Kabul.

"Hey, don't touch those!" Said Marcus the supply chief, a PFC from upstate Missouri. "Those are for the sergeant!" The chief went back to his inventory, not noticing there were a handful of strawberries missing when he went back.

Bailey found a flat rock and sat down with his improvised breakfast. He savored each strawberry, eating the little green parts, too. All in all, it was not a bad mission. He was helping the local villagers, bringing them something they needed to make a better life. He knew many of his fellow Guardsmen had signed up right after 9/11. He knew they all had their reasons: some joined as a patriotic gesture, a couple were itching for revenge, but Bailey just wanted to help people.

He had just popped his last strawberry in his mouth when

two Guardsmen came past with shovels. "Hey, c'mon," said the first one. "We gotta get this latrine dug." Bailey nodded, and headed back to his bunk to find his shovel.

The other Guardsmen at the site with Bailey were Mitchell and Higgins. They had pulled off most of their gear and laid it on the half-buried remains of an old brick wall. There was a corner of a wall, about three feet high, which disappeared into the face of the hill. The LZ perimeter fence ran right alongside the old wall for a dozen feet. Higgins had already squared off a section of ground.

"All right," said Mitchell, "let's do this thing."

The ground was hard and doughy, but with few rocks. Bailey thought it might make good planting soil.

The three of them had not worked a minute when they heard an awful, terrifying wail. They looked up, and a small, Afghan male was rushing towards them, arms waving in the air. Bailey and the others immediately looked for their weapons; they had been warned of extremists and suicide bombers. The old man, however, looked unarmed. He stopped a few paces from the Guardsmen and continued speaking to them in frenzied tones waving his arms and pointing to the ground.

"What the hell?" Higgins said finally.

"What's he saying?" Bailey asked.

The old man seemed interested in the ground they had just been digging in.

"He says not to dig there," came a voice with a heavy Afghan accent. A younger villager was coming up the gentle slope towards them. He was one of the villagers helping the other soldiers. The old man was still speaking anxious if unknown words. "He says there used to be a temple here ages ago, built by a tribe of magicians. To dig on that spot would be to anger their spirits... or something like that." The younger man came up to the old villager and put an arm around his shoulder. He spoke some words that seemed to calm the old man down. Calm or not, he still watched the soldiers with a careful eye.

"An ancient temple," said Higgins. "Great."

"You can't walk ten feet in this country without tripping over some ancient temple," added Mitchell. Bailey stepped off to his right and pointed his shovel at the ground.

"How about over here," he asked the younger Afghan. "Would over here be okay?"

"What are you doing?" Higgins asked. "We don't take orders from these camel jocks."

"Hearts and minds, dude," Bailey reminded his fellow Guardsman. "We're supposed to be working with these people, remember?" Bailey kept stepping slowly to his right. "How about now?"

The younger man translated to the old man. He calmed down, once he realized he was being listened to. He watched Bailey's footsteps carefully, and then nodded his head. "Yes," said the younger one. "That will be fine."

Bailey bowed his head. "Tell him thanks for his help." The younger villager translated, and the old man stood a little taller. He even smiled. He bowed his head in respect, and the two Afghans walked away together.

Mitchell pointed to where Bailey was standing. "You mean we gotta start all over again?"

"Hey, a hole is a hole," said Bailey, digging in the blade of his shovel. "Let's just get this thing done." The three worked in silence until the latrine was completed. The toilets themselves were on little sleds. Higgins used the Humvee to pull them over the recently-dug hole. By then, it was lunchtime. Bailey found a different MRE to eat. There were more chores to be done, vehicles to be repaired and roads to be graded. He had to gas up the Humvee for Private Walters. Apparently, there was some French bigwig in Mosul, so the brass wanted somebody who spoke French to be there. Walters was born in Louisiana and spoke fluent French, so off he went. By sunset, Bailey grabbed another bite from the mess, then headed back to his tent to try and grab some shut-eye.

He felt like he had just closed his eyes when suddenly Higgins was standing over him. "Up and at 'em, buddy!" he was saying. It was already well past dark outside. "You got guard duty tonight."

"I know, I know," Bailey said, aggravated at being awakened. He pulled on his gear and checked his rifle. They had not fired a shot in anger that whole mission, but he knew that could change in an instant. He had heard plenty of horror stories since arriving in Afghanistan. He was not about to be another statistic. Outside, the sky was a swirling mass of charcoal black clouds.

Bailey made his way to the Landing Zone. Private Foster was standing there when Bailey arrived. That didn't look right. "You here by yourself?" Bailey asked.

Foster nodded his head. "Collins is out sick."

"But, I was supposed to fill in for Collins," Bailey said.

"What can I say?" Foster said, shouldering his rifle. "I've been here since four, dude, I'm beat."

"But," Bailey said, "who's my backup? Who's supposed to be out here with me?"

"I think they had Walters lined up."

"Walters?" said Bailey. "The guy who got sent to Mosul today?"

Foster frowned. "Was that him?"

"Yeah, that was him. You mean they signed me up to fill in for one guy, but didn't get anybody for his backup?" The air was suddenly very cold. "The Sarge didn't schedule anybody else out here?"

Foster shrugged. "Looks like it. Look, dude, I'm sorry if there's been a mixup, but I'm just dead on my feet here." The wind was starting to pick up.

"But," said Bailey, "what am I supposed to do out here by myself?"

Foster held up his hands. "Take it up with the Sarge in the morning. Later." Foster walked off into the night.

Bailey sighed. *Well, crap,* he thought. He checked the lock on the LZ gate, then walked the perimeter, making sure the fence was all in one piece. That took fifteen minutes. Just another seven hours, forty-five minutes to go.

It was extremely quiet in the camp. There was a generator for running lights in camp, but the Sarge had it turned off on nights they were not expecting incoming flights. Even without electricity, he could make out the tents and vehicles by the dim light of the stars. From his position, Bailey could see the village a half mile away. He could see no lights from there, electrical or otherwise. He was not sure the remote village even had a generator for electricity. It would be nice if the Guard could leave its generator with the village when the mission was finally done. He made a mental note to suggest it to the brass in the morning.

TIM FRAYSER

Morning turned out to be a long time coming. Bailey checked his digital watch and paced out the perimeter every hour. It kept him busy. Two hours into his shift a bank of clouds crept in from the north, obscuring the stars. The clouds seemed to swirl above him in slow, swooping arcs. There had been nothing in the weather reports about storms moving in. He chalked it up to something peculiar to Afghanistan.

About three AM it got very cold. Bailey bundled up as well as he could. He did another circle of the perimeter. It helped to warm him up. Nothing was moving anywhere. Even the wind had stopped. The little American flag hanging from one of the tents was limp and motionless.

Bailey started to feel a little nervous. He had never been afraid of the dark before. On the other hand, he had never been in a war zone in the dark before. It was not completely dark. The clouds seemed to reflect whatever light there was, casting a dim, hazy glow over everything. Bailey stood completely still, listening for some kind of movement, some kind of sound. All he heard was the beating of his pulse against his temples and the rhythm of his own breathing.

Off towards the village, fog seemed to be rolling in. He could see the gentle, fuzzy glow of the fog as it came up along the ditches and dry creek beds. In the camp, it rolled in slowly around the tents. Bailey looked at the ground. Between the pebbles and dry earth, the fog came up like rising water. It rose, and pooled around Bailey's feet, forming a flat, murky surface about a foot off the ground.

Bailey frowned. This is not right, he thought. He stood completely still. The camp around him seemed to be a foot deep in fog. Did fog normally act like that? He wondered. Just then, he noticed the ancient wall off to the side, the fragment of an ancient temple the old man told them about. There was a cold breeze coming from that direction, but one that did not disturb the fog. It looked solid as glass; he could not see his feet beneath the surface. The fog came circled his legs just below the knees, and it looked like he was standing in milky water. He looked at the ancient wall, and noticed misty fog bleeding out of the broken stones. The mist rolled down the surface of the stones like a fountain and swept across the layer of fog. The mist was like oil on water, except it moved with purpose. The mist joined with the fog and swept towards Bailey's legs.

127

THE SPOOK

He tried to move, but could not. He tried to speak, but the breath seemed trapped in his lungs. Bailey watched as the misty fog surrounded him, and then began crawling up his legs. Fingers of mist reached out and climbed past his knees, his waist, moving ever upwards. He watched it come up his chest, and spread out to go down his arms. It looked like it was forming a smoky shell over his body. Bailey felt a bone-chilling cold as it moved up his back. It rose to his neck, then in a wave rushed up and over his head. Bailey trembled with fear for a moment, then his lungs erupted with a loud, "Aaa!"

At once, the shell of mist broke up, and expanded away from his body, dissipating into the night air. At his feet, the fog separated away from his legs, like the calm surface of a pond expanding in ripples. The fog swept away from him, retreating behind the tents and vehicles, sweeping across the rocky plain and draining away into the ditches and dry creek beds. In moments, there was no trace of it anywhere.

"Hey!" someone cried out. The voice made Bailey jump. It was Higgins, peeking out from a tent flap. "What is your problem?"

Bailey cleared his throat. "Um," he said, stomping a booted foot, "just trying to stay awake."

Higgins rolled his eyes and shook his head, which disappeared back into the tent.

Bailey took a deep breath to calm himself. He looked around. There was no fog anywhere, even way over towards the village. Above, the swirling clouds even seemed to be breaking up. Stars appeared. He coughed. Adjusting the sling of his weapon, he turned to make another circuit of the perimeter.

Morning came, and when his relief finally arrived, Bailey went back to his tent. It took him a long time to fall asleep, lying in his tent, staring straight up. He never complained to the Sergeant about the lone duty, never made any reports about the weather, and certainly never mentioned the strange fog to anyone. He was not sure he had not imagined it. Could he have fallen asleep on duty, and dreamed the whole thing? He tried to purge the entire experience from his memory.

The next day, however, was even colder. A front moved

in, blocking out the sun all day and bringing a bitter wind. Duties were cut short as the Guardsmen just tried to stay warm. Bailey wished he had more duties. He needed to keep busy, to take his mind off the mysterious fog. When the Sarge asked for volunteers to dig more irrigation ditches, Bailey jumped at the chance.

Rest, however, turned out elusive on that rugged Afghan plain. The sky got darker as the day wore on. That night was brutally cold. The front had moved in with frigid temperatures. There were reports of snow to the north. The Guardsmen hunkered down as best they could. PFC Marcus got a burn barrel going, but it was not quite warm enough. The night just kept getting colder. The Guardsmen ended up in their tents, huddled in their bunks.

Winter in Afghanistan sucks! Bailey thought. He had the flaps of his tent weighed down with rocks, but that did little to keep the frigid air from invading. It swept in and filled the tent like a refrigerator. Bailey put on every stitch of clothing he had and piled everything else on top of his sleeping bag. He huddled inside the cocoon, shivering against the cold. Above, the top of the tent flapped in the wind. Even if he was warm, the continuous noise from the wind would keep him awake.

Bailey closed his eyes. He knew from experience it did not matter what was going on around him—if he was tired enough, he could fall asleep anywhere. He just had to wait until he got tired enough. He listened to the constant flapping of the tent and tried to think warm thoughts. He found himself thinking of warmer places, happier times... like the time his parents took him on that trip to the Grand Canyon. That was a great trip.

It was the last summer his parents were together. They were still talking to each other at that point. He was in first grade and crazy about dinosaurs, so when they stopped at the Painted Desert his folks bought him a real dinosaur fossil. He carried it around for years. He had it with him when they spent the night in Flagstaff, there on the nightstand next to the bed with the stiff sheets. The hotel had no air conditioning, for some reason, so they all slept on top of those stiff sheets with the windows open. It did not matter.

He took the fossil with him when they drove north the next morning, through mountains and forests and across a fantastic desert plain. It was already hot out by mid-morning. There was a campground with Flintstones characters, but then they got to the visitor's center, which had more dinosaur bones. His mom bought him a toy stegosaurus. He had it with him when they went out to see the canyon itself.

Snuggled in his bunk, Bailey felt warmer already as the memories of that trip rushed back to him. He remembered his mom wanted to get a bite to eat, but his dad wanted to see the canyon first. He forgot all about dinosaurs when they came around that corner and saw the Grand Canyon for the first time, spreading out before them as far as the eye could see. He carefully went up to the rail and looked down. The canyon went down and down until he thought it was going to go to the center of the earth. As impressive as the sight was, what Bailey really remembered was the sound: the sound of the wind as it came over the canyon. It was like nothing he had ever heard. It was not a rush, or a roar, it was more like...

A sigh. A great, majestic sigh, as if God Himself had looked upon His works and exhaled a breath of contentment for all to hear. Bailey breathed deep, as if he could hear that magnificent, sighing wind once more...

...And, oddly enough, that was exactly what he heard. The constant flapping of the tent had stopped, replaced by the satisfied breeze of his youth. Bailey realized he was no longer cold. In fact, he was hot, and there was a light in his eyes.

"What the—?" he said to himself as his eyes blinked open. The light was blinding and warm, and something was stabbing him in the hand, the side, the back of his neck! "Ow! Ow!" he cried, as he realized he was being stabbed in several places. He pushed himself upright, his hands landing on sharp objects at every touch. Bailey scrambled to his feet, blinking madly at the light. His foot came across a stone and he fell hard on his side. The flat surface was hot, searing, and Bailey rolled away until he came against something high and solid.

He caught his breath, and slowly his eyesight returned. The stars in his eyes stopped flashing. It was not as hot any more. He found himself in the shade, up against a stone wall. The hot surface was concrete—a sidewalk. There was blood on his fingers. His hands and neck hurt from multiple small cuts. Bailey's eyes focused. There was a bright, hot sun shining down on him from a clear blue sky.

He sat up, his back to the stone wall. He was still wearing his BDU pants, and his t-shirt, but all the other clothes he went to bed with were gone. He was barefoot, sitting next to a hot sidewalk, injured and in pain. "What—where—?" he whispered to himself. The air carried the scents of pine and juniper. He took a deep breath...

And that was when he heard it. The sigh. The majestic, global sigh. Bailey stood of shaky legs and turned around. On the other side of the short stone wall, the ground extended another five feet, then dropped off into oblivion. Beyond, the earth twisted and rose in a hundred colors of the rainbow all the way to the horizon.

Bailey tried to swallow; his throat dry. The Grand Canyon. He was back. He was back at the Grand Canyon.

He shook his head. A dream. It had to be a dream. But it was unlike any dream he had ever had. It looked so real. It felt real. He looked at his hands, cut and scratched. Bailey looked back at the patch of cactus and yucca he had been lying in, and shook his head. Why would I dream about lying in cactus? he thought. That did not make sense. Why would I feel pain?

Still, a sense of peace rose inside him. For years, he had dreamed about going back to the Grand Canyon, but he never seemed to have the time. He reached out and touched the top of the stone wall. It was rough and warm, heated by the sun. He looked down at his bare feet. The concrete was warm, but the breeze was cool. He blinked. He did not remember it being that cool at the canyon. Bailey looked down the stone wall, which ran along the canyon rim. He frowned. He remembered looking through a railing that ran along the canyon rim, not a stone wall.

About forty yards down the wall, a family was enjoying the view. Two parents and a child. Only, they were wearing jackets. Long sleeves. The little boy even had a stocking cap on. A chill went down Bailey's arms. It was the middle of summer when he was here. The family turned to leave. The little boy turned and saw Bailey. He waved, and Bailey waved back. As he lowered his hand, he noticed a small plaque imbedded in the stone wall. It stated the wall was constructed as an improvement process. It gave a date. The date was years after Bailey and his family had visited.

Bailey's breath became heavy in his chest. This was no dream, he thought. He was really there, at the Grand Canyon—not in the past, as he remembered, but in the present, in the now, the middle of winter. He looked back out across the canyon. Patches of snow could be seen on some of the higher buttes. Bailey ran a hand across his face. How was this possible?

No, he decided—it had to be a dream. It had to be! Bailey took off running. He ran as fast as his bare feet could carry him along the canyon rim path. It just went on and on. Sweat appeared on his face. The stones hurt his bare feet; he did not care. He ran past two teenagers, holding hands. The path twisted and turned as he followed it down the rim. He was gasping for air when he finally stopped. He bent over, hands on knees, trying to catch his breath. He was still there! He was still in Arizona, at the damn Grand Canyon! He held his face with his hands. This can't be happening! He thought of his buddies in the Guard, the camp, LZ 465... the stones of the ancient temple. He frowned. Surely that could not—-

And suddenly, the lights went out. Everything around him turned black. A gust of wind blew a handful of dust into Bailey's face. He blinked, and when his eyes focused, he was still outside, but it was night. The canyon was gone. He was standing barefoot on rocky ground, next to one of the personnel trucks. Above, the American flag flapped vigorously in the wind. He was back. He was in the camp again—and suddenly very cold. He hurried back to his tent, looking over his shoulder the whole time.

Safely inside, he grabbed the top blanket off his bunk and wrapped himself in it. He sat on the hard floor, knees to his chest, the blanket pulled tight around him.

It was a dream after all. Just a dream. A crazy, crazy dream. He was dreaming all along—and sleepwalking! He was outside in his sleep. When did he start sleepwalking? He hoped no one saw him outside. People got thrown out of the military for sleepwalking. He heard no one, saw no one. Nobody called out to him. He was safe.

He looked at his hands, his feet. They were bloody, scraped-up... from running down the canyon rim, waking up in a cactus patch. No! He shook his head. That must have happened when he went sleepwalking. He was sleepwalking in his bare feet and that was when he got scratched-up. That was the only logical explanation.

He took a deep breath to relax. Sleep. He needed to sleep. He stood, and went to his bunk. It was still untouched. The covers were right where he had piled them. He pulled the blankets aside. There, at the bottom, was his BDU shirt, laid out and buttoned-up, just like it was on him when he went to bed. He pulled the blankets aside at the foot of the bunk. There were his socks, lying right where his feet had been.

That was... odd.

He felt a chill and climbed under the covers. As he reclined, something sharp stuck him in the back. He sat up and pulled it out. It was something small. He had to grab his flashlight to see what it was.

It was a thorn. A cactus thorn.

"What the hell?" said Bailey out loud. "What. The. Hell...?!?"

THE SPOOK

CHAPTER 22 – SATURDAY AFTERNOON

La Estrella was the last station on the Autopista Regional rail line on the southwest end of Medellin. The narrow Medellin River surged past the north side of the small complex. Warehouses lined the streets south of the station. The doors of one warehouse were open this day, fresh air passing through the curtain of rain into the expanse within.

Inside, the darkness of the warehouse concealed determined activity. Soldiers in uniforms checked weapons, pulled on body armor, and gassed up vehicles. Something important was imminent, Johnson observed, as he walked in from the rain.

The familiar face passed easily by guards and the door to the upstairs office opened for him. General Gomez had used this warehouse as a staging point for many raids. Today, he sat behind the map-covered desk, loading his black .357 magnum.

"Busy day," Johnson observed.

"Important day," Gomez corrected. He put the gun down and wiped his hands on a small towel. "Today will mark the end of El Marinaro's reign in Columbia. And this victory will be the last triumph I need for my new political career."

Johnson nodded. "Congratulations, in advance," he said. "Getting rid of Bravo will indeed be a feather in your cap, but may I offer some advice?"

"Of course, mi amigo. Drink?"

"Please," Johnson nodded. "I say only: Why stop at one feather when you can get two?"

Gomez stopped in mid-pour to look at Johnson. "What do you mean?"

Johnson pointed to the land line on the desk. "You are waiting for El Gancho's call, are you not? To tell you the coast is clear?"

Gomez smiled, then let out a laugh. He set Johnson's drink down on the desk. "Not much gets past you, amigo, eh?"

THE SPOOK

Johnson shrugged. "I hear things." He accepted the glass of whiskey. "What I mean is, why get only Bravo when you can take two players out of the game?"

Gomez nodded, understanding. "El Gancho."

"Precisely. He will already be on the premises, correct? He already has a long association with Bravo, and should he take over Bravo's business, as I presume he intends, he will more than likely be a ... liability to you."

Gomez thought for a moment. "Whereas you would not be? How do I know you would not take over Bravo's enterprise with the two of them out of the way?"

"Oh, I have plans for the future," Johnson said, "but they do not involve heroin or cocaine. My retirement plan lies with other investments, ones that you do not need to concern yourself with."

Johnson took a sip, and looked out the window at the falling rain. "To be honest, I grow weary of this life, working for commission, going from job to job, working for someone else. San Cordero will be the perfect place for me to settle down, maybe start a family of my own."

A knock at the door made both men look. A lieutenant stood at the entrance to the office. "All is ready, mi general."

Gomez nodded and waved the young man away. "Yes, I would have thought you'd be on your way by now," Johnson observed.

The general nodded to the window. A train rumbled in the distance. "Not in the rain," he said. "I do not like getting my uniform wet. It makes me look fat. Newspaper photos can be so unflattering. As soon as the rain moves through, we attack. Another drink?"

Johnson waved away the offer, standing. "I have a flight to catch. Remember my suggestion, general. In the long run, I think you will agree I am right." Johnson nodded goodbye and left the room.

The general thought for a moment, then made a decision. He opened a file cabinet and pulled out a thick folder. He marched out to the warehouse floor to a wide bulletin board near the exit. Maps of the area were tacked on the board, along with a photo of Valentin Bravo. It was under a standing order to Gomez's troops: *disparar sin previo aviso*, "shoot without

136

warning." Anyone targeted by this order was to be killed on sight, no questions asked. Next to Bravo's photo, Gomez tacked a photo of Antonio Lopez, El Gancho.

Gomez thought about the wisdom of Johnson's words. Disposing of El Marinaro and El Gancho together in one fell swoop would make life much simpler. It was an intriguing proposition. It would, as El Gancho himself would agree, wipe the slate clean.

THE SPOOK

CHAPTER 23 – SATURDAY AFTERNOON

Everything was a blur. Bailey had a sensation of movement, of being pulled out of the cab into the rain, of being carried. Raindrops splattered on his chest. His body felt fuzzy, out of step. Things changed, and he felt he must be riding in some vehicle. His ears wouldn't stop ringing. Slowly, the blurry images came into focus.

The vehicle bounced, and his head rolled to one side. Beyond the window, Bailey thought he must have arrived at some French chateau. Groves of gardens and green lawns fell before them. Off in the distance was a large, white mansion, built halfway up a hill. As the road got closer to the house, he could see a dock just below the mansion. There were two smaller boats and one long, powerful speedboat tied up at the dock.

The mansion dominated the scene, something like the big house in *Gone with the Wind*: white pillars lined the front, with wide, white steps leading up to the front doors. The vehicle passed by those steps and rolled around to the far side of the mansion. The vehicle stopped, and the doors opened. Bailey found himself dragged out into the rain again. He managed to find his feet and stumbled as he was pushed into a long, white building.

He was pushed to his knees inside the breezy structure. He lurched forward, landing on his hands. There was a line of expensive cars parks off to the left. To his right were racks of tools and boxes of car parts. He felt sick to his stomach and laid down on the cold concrete.

He seemed to be floating in a dream. The concrete floor was no dream. It was right there, pressing against his cheek. He opened his eyes, took a deep breath, and got a dizzy, lopsided view of people's feet. Off to the side he could see cans of gasoline lined up along the wall.

"What do we do with him?" he heard someone say.

"The boss wants to see him," another voice replied.

THE SPOOK

He felt hands against his body, lifting him up, and the pain came back, stabbing deep into his neck and head. He gasped at the pain, which just became more acute the more he woke up. More voices; they hummed and echoed and bounced around in his ears. He could not move his hands. He realized his wrists were bound in handcuffs.

More talking. Hands grabbed at him again. This time, he knew to keep his head steady as he was lifted to his feet. It was no longer raining when they took him outside. He was led past a small white-washed building, possibly a gardener's shed. In through a side door, they passed through the wide kitchen. Modern appliances lined the walls. He could smell fresh bread baking. Servants averted their eyes. Up two flights of dark stairs and down a dark hallway, Bailey tried to not look too awake. He was dropped hard on the expensive, carpeted floor.

"¿Cuál es éste?" came a crisp, cultured voice.

Bailey rose on his elbows to look up. He was in a paneled study, with shelves of books rising to the ceiling. Rich, carved wood decorated every corner of the room. Expensive-looking portraits hung on the walls. In front of him was a hand-carved mahogany desk; it looked very old. A man was walking out from behind it. The Latino man looked to be in his fifties. He wore white slacks and a comfortable Hawaiian shirt. He looked down on Bailey with distain. "Who is this who tries to invade my home?" Bailey squinted up at the stout man. "Trespassing is a serious charge. Do you know who I am?"

Bailey's head throbbed as he was catching his breath. He looked around the plush room. "You're the man in charge."

Valentin Bravo grinned. "Indeed I am, amigo. In ways you cannot comprehend. Now, tell me why you were on my property?"

Bailey coughed. "Just passing through, is all."

Benito stepped forward. "He was messing around the canister from the airport, Senor Johnson's canister."

Bravo sighed. "Ah, now that is a problem, my gringo friend. Investments must be protected, you understand. Do you represent one of my rivals, a competitor, perhaps? One of my enemies? Who sent you to my house?"

Bailey lowered his head slowly. It hurt to keep looking up. "Nobody sent me," he replied.

One of the gunmen came forward and gave Bailey a swift kick to the thigh. The blow rolled him over, and he squirmed on the carpeted floor. "Look at Mr. Bravo when you're being talked to!" yelled the gunman.

Bravo held up one hand, and the gunman stepped away from Bailey. "Our quiet saboteur wants to play games. So be it." He looked at his watch and crossed to the office door. "I have too much business today to attend to. Benito," he called. "Please take this person downstairs and find out what he knows. Who sent him. Then ...dispose of him. And do not wake my daughter."

"Yes, sir, Mr. Bravo," Benito said. Hands grabbed Bailey by the neck and pulled him to his feet.

"Come along, gringo!" Benito snarled, pushing him towards the door. Hands on either side grabbed him by the elbows and hurried him along down a different flight of stairs. Bailey's head was clearing quickly. He counted at least six gunmen escorting him. As the stairs traveled down, the opulence of the upper levels faded. The mansion's lowest level was simple grey, concrete walls and floors. There was a line of plain steel doors. One was opened, and Bailey was taken inside.

It was the size of a small office: grey walls with one window on the far end. A steel table sat in the middle of the room, surrounded by steel chairs. Bailey was taken to the head of the table, directly under the sole window, set down roughly while one man produced a length of rope. He wrapped it around Bailey's waist, tying him to the chair.

The one called Benito closed the door. The others stood around the table, looking down on their prisoner with expressions of extreme distaste. The pain in his head had faded to a dull throb, but his mind had cleared. Bailey cleared his throat.

"Hey," Bailey said quietly. "You guys wanna see a magic trick?"

The men eyed him suspiciously, their eyes slits of fire. "Oh, c'mon," Bailey said. "Looks like we're gonna be here a while. Let's pass the time. C'mon, give me a quarter and I'll show you a magic trick. Or a nickel. Really, any coin will do."

One by one, the fierce characters looked at Benito. The

pony-tailed man examined the prisoner closely, and finally smiled. "Sure. Why not? You," he pointed to one of his men. "Give him a coin." The man pulled out a coppery-looking coin and tossed it to Bailey. He caught it with difficulty, the handcuffs on his hands jingling. The coin read twenty pesos.

"Okay, everybody sit down," he directed. Nobody moved. "Oh, come on, you wanna see a trick or not?"

The one called Benito shook his head, chuckling under his breath. "Very well, senor. We will sit down. Amigos, come, let us all sit down for the gringo's magic trick." The men all sat down at the long table, Benito at the far end, opposite Bailey. Bailey recognized Benito's short friend from before, eyeing him suspiciously, sitting to Benito's right.

Bailey turned the coin over in his exposed fingers. "You're gonna like this," he said with a smile. "This is a very intense form of magic, taught to me by a powerful magician from Egypt—"

"Will you get on with it, senor?" Benito said loudly.

"Sure, sure," the prisoner said. He held up the coin in one shackled hand. "Can everybody see this? Are you sitting where you can all see the coin?" They all nodded. Benito rolled his eyes.

"Okay, now, this trick only works if everybody keeps their eye on the coin," he said, looking down the line at the gunmen's faces. "I'm gonna toss this up into the air, and you've all got to watch it. You've got to keep your eyes on the coin the whole time it's in the air. Understand?" They all nodded yes again. Bailey smiled.

"What is going to happen?" one of the gunmen asked.

"Well, if I told you, it wouldn't be a surprise, would it?"

The others laughed at their companion.

"Okay, everybody ready?" Bailey's tongue appeared at the corner of his mouth as he concentrated on the coin. He then brought his hands together and flipped the coin into the air with his thumb. He reached out to the extent his bounds would let him and retrieved the coin. "All right," he said with a smile. "You guys are gonna like this!" He looked up, brought his hands together once again, and flipped the coin into the air again.

The coin went much higher than before, almost to the

ceiling, then came straight down. It hit the table and loudly bounced twice before spinning on its edge. The men all gasped with astonishment, not because of the coin, but because their prisoner was—gone! His chair was empty; the rope that had been tied around his waist hung loose on the chair. The handcuffs that had been on his wrists lay on the table in front of where he had been sitting. Even the chair had not moved. The prisoner had simply disappeared.

Benito and his men stared in disbelief. They pushed themselves away from the table and looked underneath. "Madre di Dios!" one man exclaimed, crossing himself. Benito was speechless. He jumped up, knocking his own chair over, and rushed to the prisoner's chair. He picked it up to look underneath.

"Don't just stand there!" he cried at the others, tossing the prisoner's chair into the corner. "Spread out! Search the grounds! Find him! Find him!" The men scrambled for the door.

The only one that remained sitting was Estiban, who calmly looked up at Benito. "I told you he was a witch."

Reappearing on Bravo's expensive carpet, Bailey spun around. He found himself alone—for the moment. There were voices in the hallway. Bailey quickly moved to the door and carefully closed it. There was no lock. Behind him, the room was empty. Winking back upstairs to Bravo's private office was a huge risk. He gambled that Bravo was the kind of man that did not approve of people puttering around his private office while he was away, but Bailey had to take the chance. After coming all that way, he was determined to find something to use against Bravo.

He set the timer on his watch and returned to Bravo's desk. There were papers scattered around; papers with rows of numbers, lists of names. There were spreadsheets, pie charts, statements, and official-looking letters on expensive stationery. But—everything was in Spanish. He couldn't tell if they were important or not. He folded a handful of papers in his gloved hands and stuffed them in his pockets.

In the top right-hand drawer of the desk he found stack of pictures colored in crayon. Beneath those was a loaded Baretta automatic. There was a calendar on the desk, with dates circled and X-ed-out. Directly next to it was a small pocket-sized spiral notebook. There were hand-written notes on every page he flipped through. He pocketed that as well.

Bailey's hand was still in his pocket when he looked up. There was a second door to the room, off to the side behind a pair of chairs. Standing in the open door was a little girl, maybe six years old. She had jet black hair, straight bangs across her forehead, and wore a white linen dress. Bailey froze. It was too soon for him to blink away. There was no place for him to go. If she raised an alarm there would be no escape.

He smiled at the girl. She said nothing. He realized how he must look, filthy and caked in mud, anachronistic against the backdrop of the luxurious room. He slowly raised one hand to wave. The girl responded with a little wave of her own. That was encouraging.

Bailey thought of the school groups that routinely came through the library. He had no trouble talking to them, but did this girl even speak English? "Habla Engles?" he asked quietly.

The girl shook her head. Bailey felt very vulnerable. The door behind her was open, and anyone could walk by and see him. There were lots of people walking around with guns and he didn't want to meet up with them. He pointed to the door, then brought his hands up in front of him. Slowly, he brought them together.

The girl opened her mouth, as if to say something, then closed it. She nodded her head. Silently, she backed out of the room and closed the door behind her. Bailey was alone. That was weird, he thought. He glanced at his watch. Still time to kill... if it didn't kill him first.

He looked over the papers scattered across the desk. There were letters, printouts of tables, pictures of ships and buildings. Most of it was in Spanish. The information on the spreadsheets meant nothing to Bailey, but he had no doubt they were important. He shoved them into the pockets of the BDU shirt.

Bailey froze. Footsteps. Someone was coming down the hallway. He could hear a man speaking, talking to someone, but no responses. Bailey realized the man must be talking on his phone.

Gancho had to hold the phone away from his head. The yelling was hurting his ears. "Senor, senor, calm down."

"I will not calm down!" Johnson replied. He stood beside his private helicopter, a chilly wind blowing across the tarmac. In spite of Gancho's words, he took a breath before speaking again. "I'm at the airport in Medellin. I just spoke to the captain of the Wushu Senator," he said slowly. "The ship is refueling in Gibraltar, and he says my package never got on the ship!"

"That is true, senor," Gancho said. "Mr. Shamoun redirected the shipment without authorization."

"Shamoun! Why the hell would he do that?"

"To impress El Marinaro, he said. But do not worry. He has been properly disciplined."

"Never mind that!" spat Johnson. "Where is the package? Is it on another ship?"

"No, no, senor. It is safe. It is here."

"Here," repeated Johnson. "Here, as in Columbia?"

"Here as in... here, senor," Gancho replied simply. "San Cordero. Senor Bravo's estate."

Johnson gasped. He thought of Gomez and his raiding party. Guns blazing, clumsy, trigger-happy soldiers would destroy everything. "No!" he breathed. "Why—? Never mind!" He turned to the pilot, watching him from inside the helicopter. Johnson twirled a finger in the air, the order to start the engines. "Never mind!" he yelled into the phone. "I'll take care of this myself! Bloody hell!"

Gancho shrugged. "As you wish, senor." He disconnected the call as one of the hired men came around the corner.

"No sign of the gringo, boss," he reported.

"Keep looking!" Gancho growled. "Send men into the jungle and secure the docks."

"Right away, boss," the man replied

As the man left, Gancho's fingers swiped across his phone until he found the correct number. It rang once. "Yes?"

"Ah, mi general," Gancho said. "The guards have been called from the gates, searching for some trespasser. You may begin your operation."

"Thank you, amigo," replied Gomez.

Gancho smiled to himself as he disconnected. He knew the location of Gomez's facility in Medillin. There would be plenty of time for him to exit the grounds before the excitement started; plausible deniability. "Everything is in progress. Soon, todo esto será mío." He turned, and spotted Bravo's daughter standing at the end of the hallway.

"Well, hello, little one," Gancho said with a smile. "You haven't seen a loco gringo around here, have you?"

"Only the one in Papa's office," the girl said.

Gancho's smile faded. "What?" He stared at the door for a moment, then pushed past the girl, drawing his pistol. Gancho swung the door open and burst into the room, gun raised, searching the walls with his eyes. The room was empty. He stood motionless for a moment, listening. Satisfied the girl must have been playing a trick on him, Gancho was about to put his gun away when he heard a sound: a tiny, mechanical buzzing, like some kind of alarm. It was coming from behind the door. Gancho advanced to the door.

Gun in hand, Gancho pulled the door aside to reveal—only the empty wall. He shook his head at such foolishness. Stuffing his gun back in his waistband, he chuckled to himself as he left the office, pulling the door shut behind him. He never saw the muddy footprints on the floor.

Miles away, Gomez put the cellphone back into his breast pocket. The Jeep bounced along the backroads leading to San Cordero. Behind him, the trucks of soldiers followed close behind. There was no way for Gancho to know Gomez had forwarded calls from his Medillin number to his cellphone, no way for Gancho to know he was so close. The operation to stop Bravo—and Gancho—was well underway.

CHAPTER 24 – SATURDAY AFTERNOON

...And Bailey was in his bathroom. The light from the window shone across the white tile floor. That was close, he thought. In the mirror, he looked terrible. His hair was muddy, his face was bruised, and his left eye was beginning to swell. He reset his watch. Bailey leaned wearily on the sink. He needed to clean up, and pee, but he needed to sit down more. He walked slowly out into the hall leading to the living room. Everything was exactly as he left it that morning. He sat down heavily on the couch and let his head roll back to rest on the cushions. It felt good to be not moving. Or getting beat up. Or being shot at.

With a grunt, he sat up and began unlacing his boots. He set them aside to start drying out. Once off, he peeled away his soaked socks and wiggled his toes. They felt good, exposed to the air. He propped his feet up on the coffee table.

He heard a buzzing sound. It was his smart phone, which he'd left connected to the recharger. He pushed himself up off the couch. Barefoot, he walked over to the end table and picked it up. There was a missed call and several text messages, all from the same number. The area code was 757: Virginia. Van Brunt, the CIA lady, he concluded. He scrolled down through texts, each more insistent than the last—the last of which read, in all caps, NEED TO SEE YOU NOW!

Bailey sighed, and typed out a reply and sent it. He checked his watch. He decided he needed some aspirin. And some dry socks. Food would be good, too...

At CIA headquarters in Langley, Weaver was in the conference room waiting for a satellite up-link to bring the live feed of the carrier group in the Caribbean. A strike force had been assembled to move in if necessary, with troops and air support. Several others were in the room, working on their laptops.

A man entered the room and went directly to Weaver. "Sir,"

he said, "we have word General Gomez and his strike team are in the process of conducting a drug raid."

Weaver said, "A raid against whom? Who's the target?"

"Unknown," the man said. "But his troops have just left Medillin, the convoy headed east."

Weaver looked at a map spread out across the table. "Bravo's estate?"

The man shrugged. "Possible. They've been silent running since leaving the city."

Tabitha stood at the door, and listened to the conversation. She had read reports of Gomez's raids before: massacre was more like it. It was his style. He was a "Shoot 'em all, let God sort 'em out" kind of guy. Her fingers tapped the cellphone in her hand, impatiently, as she watched the bustling work. She was about to send another text when it buzzed in her hand. Forcing herself to act casual, she slipped out of the room and hurried to the women's restroom. Tabitha locked herself into a stall and opened up her message app.

It read, Public place. No cameras. Send picture. Come alone.

Tabitha rushed back to her cubicle to grab her jacket and purse.

"What's going on, Tabitha?" Agent Reed asked, who was sitting in the next cubicle, a laptop balanced on his knees.

"I gotta get out for a while," she said. "Get some fresh air."

Reed nodded. "Let us know if you find any." He went back to his laptop.

Tabitha walked quickly out of the building, through security checkpoints, and got into her car. She pulled out of the parking garage, flashed her credentials, and was out on the highway to—where was she going? Some public place, he said. Tabitha kept looking in her rear-view mirror, to see if she was being followed, but the people she worked for were experts at not being seen. She had to take the chance. It was a bright, sunny day. She was on the Washington Parkway, which ran along the Potomac River. Not much there, she thought, but then she started seeing exit signs, and knew where she had to go.

Arlington National Cemetery was only eight miles from

CIA headquarters, directly across the river from the Lincoln Memorial. Tabitha could see the Washington Monument off in the distance as she pulled off the highway. She exited at Memorial Drive and pulled into the cemetery. She had been there only once before, when she first moved to Virginia. Finding a parking place was maddening, but she found a spot, hurried out, and started walking. There were too many people around.

She walked past the administration building, and passed more cars, which she figured was employee parking. She crossed Eisenhower Drive, and finally stood before acres and acres of white stones, the graves stretching off in all directions. A sign told her she was in Section 33. She marched deep into the lines of stones, surrounded by hallowed ground.

She stopped to look around, and confident there was no one else in sight, and no security cameras watching, she took out her phone and took a picture. It took her several clicks to call up Bailey's number and send it. Tabitha looked at her phone, and slowly slipped it back into her purse, thinking how ridiculous it must look for her—

"About time."

Tabitha whirled around, and there was Bailey, standing not fifteen feet away from her. A gloved hand resting on top of a marble headstone. He wore the black BDU shirt she remembered from the Interpol pictures, the shirttails flapping in the gentle breeze. It was a dramatic change from the last time they met. Bailey's face was bruised, his hair dirty and disheveled, his eyes weary and frustrated.

"You look like hell," Tabitha blurted out.

Bailey nodded. "Nice to see you, too," he said sarcastically. He casually looked around in all directions.

"We're alone," she said. "You said alone."

"You told them, didn't you? You told them about me."

"What? No! No, I didn't—"

"Is this a recruitment trip? Are the black helicopters coming to take me away? Is a sniper with a tranquilizer gun hiding out there somewhere? To make me do some spook job for the spymasters? To get me to be a spook?"

"No, I swear," Tabitha said, trying to make her voice sound calm. "It's just me. Just me. That's all."

Bailey relaxed. "What do you want?"

Tabitha stepped forward. "I need to know what else you heard in that junkyard in Columbia," she said quickly. "The one where you got shot."

"I remember," he said. "I just came from there."

"What, Columbia? You were there... today?"

"About an hour ago."

Thousands of miles away, an hour ago, Tabitha thought. It was mind-boggling. Despite the sunlight, she felt a chill down her back. "What—what were you doing in Columbia?"

"Getting chased, shot at, beaten up. I went back looking for those killers. I also... broke somebody's truck." He looked away, his face shrouded with guilt. "Okay, I didn't break it, but it's broken and it's my fault. I've got to make it up to him, somehow."

"Did you find them? The killers?"

"Oh, yeah," he said. "And their boss; Bravo, right?"

"Yes, Valentin Bravo, AKA El Marinaro," she said. She stared at his bruised face. "You actually saw him? In person?"

"He had his goons take me away, but I blinked out on them. Oh, that reminds me." He reached into his pockets and pulled out several sheets of paper, haphazardly folded and crumbled. He handed them over to Tabitha. "I got these from Bravo's desk. They might not mean anything, but there might be something useful in there. There's this, too." He pulled out the pocket notebook and handed it over. "Take it all. Because there's no way I'm going back there."

Tabitha stared blindly at the wads of paper in her hands. Papers from a drug lord's desk across the hemisphere. "What was it you wanted again?" he asked.

She shook her head. "You said you heard them say 'Shenzhen.' The men in the junkyard. Did they say where it was?" Tabitha started cramming the papers into her purse.

Bailey thought. "The airport. It was supposed to be on a boat, but Shamoun, the guy they shot, put it on a plane instead." He looked around the cemetery, finally satisfied they were alone. The sunlight was drying out the mud on his clothes. Despite the dry socks, his feet felt strange inside the damp boots.

"Shamoun," Tabitha said, staring out across the stones. "He sent word to the Consulate about the Shenzhen," she said, thinking out loud. "And he rerouted the package, giving us time to act on it." She looked up at Bailey. "He knew how dangerous Shinzhen was. He was trying to stop it. And they killed him for it. Him and his son, and his wife Shea."

Bailey sighed heavily. "Was that her name?" he asked quietly. Tabitha nodded her head. Bailey looked off to the trees. "What is it, exactly? The stuff? What's it do?"

Tabitha took a deep breath. She was about to break the law. "*Shinzhen Wu.* From China. It's an aerosol contraceptive, a gas that keeps women from getting pregnant. That's what it was for originally. It's been weaponized into something that can sterilize a person. Enough of it can sterilize a population. It was supposed to be something for family planning. Now it's a terrorist weapon."

Bailey frowned. "Why would Bravo want stuff like that?"

"To sell to terrorists, extremists, fanatics—anybody that wanted to wipe out a population... My God, he must already have buyers, people standing by to use the stuff right away..."

"Christ," said Bailey suddenly, looking at his gloved hand. "I think I touched it."

"What? No," Tabitha said. "It's in transit somewhere. We think it's being transported in a pressurized tank—"

"A tank about yay big?" Bailey asked, holding his hand level right over his forehead. He then held his hands out slightly beyond the width of his shoulders. "And this wide? Chinese characters painted on the side?"

Tabitha gasped. "Oh, my God... That must be it. You've seen it? Where? Where is it?"

"It was on a truck when I was sneaking into Bravo's property," Bailey said. "A big pressurized tank, right? If it was on a plane they must have boxed it up first—hey," he remembered. "They said it had to be kept under 39 degrees, but, it gets way hotter than that in Columbia."

Tabitha snapped her fingers. "Celsius. Thirty-nine degrees Celsius," she said. "About a hundred degrees Fahrenheit."

"What happens if it gets hotter than that?"

Tabitha opened her mouth, then closed it. "I don't know," she admitted. "But contents under pressure have to be kept within certain limits, for safety reasons."

"It was on a truck," Bailey said, "like it was tractor parts or something. If they were bouncing that thing around the countryside, they might crack the casing, cause a leak. Heck, it could be leaking right now."

Tabitha ran a hand across her mouth. "Okay, okay," she said, calming herself down. "The Navy has a strike force ready to move in and grab the stuff..."

"Well then, great," said Bailey. "The Marines grab the stuff, secure the perimeter, stop the bad guys, good guys win... right?"

Tabitha was shaking her head. "I don't think my bosses are going to send in the Marines," she said slowly.

Bailey frowned. "Why the hell not?"

"A guy from the Pentagon," Tabitha said, pacing between the stones. "Okay, maybe he doesn't represent everybody, maybe they won't listen to him, but... Shinzhen would be a game-changer, a tactical weapon of deterrence... but the world would have to see it in action first."

"Oh, hell," Bailey said. "They're gonna let these assholes go ahead and use it? On people?"

Tabitha looked up in shame. "Maybe. There's also a chance Gomez might capture it for himself. Use it for his own political agenda."

Bailey cocked his head. "Who's Gomez?"

"General Gomez, Columbian anti-drug enforcer. He's making a move today but we don't know against whom."

"So he might get to Bravo before the Marines?" Bailey asked. "Is that a good thing?"

Tabitha shook her head. "Gomez is ruthless. He's known for killing everyone in sight, taking no prisoners, all in the name of making his country a better place. If he launches an assault on Bravo... it'll be a slaughter."

Bailey frowned, and took a step backwards. "No, no, no, there's innocent people there, workers—kids!" He thought of the little girl in the doorway, not much younger than the little boy killed in the junkyard. "No, you can't let that happen. You gotta send the Marines in, make them get there first and catch this Shinzhen stuff! You gotta make the call and send in the troops! You gotta make the call!"

"Columbian troops, American troops, Bravo's men won't give it up without a fight," Tabitha sighed, her eyes distant and sad. "No matter what happens, there's bound to be... collateral damage."

Bailey's eyes narrowed; his gloved hand slapped the top of a tombstone. "Not on my watch!"

She watched him turn to walk away. "Wait, where are you going!" she cried. "You said you weren't going back there!"

Bailey kept walking.

"What can you do? You can't even take a gun with you! You're just one person!"

Bailey did not look back.

Tabitha looked at her watch. They'd be wondering where she went back at the office. "Dammit!" she spat as she rushed back towards her car.

One person, Bailey thought. One person might make a difference, even if it's only to save one little girl's life. He kept walking, straight through the rows of marble stones, and thought of baked bread...

THE SPOOK

CHAPTER 25 – LATE SATURDAY AFTERNOON

Consuela opened the oven door, and the heat reached out for her face. Mitts in hand, she pulled out the pans of freshly-baked bread. She stood, and turned to put the pans on the table. Turning back, she started to pull the mitts off her hands but was startled by the sudden appearance of a man next to the stove.

"Por dios!" Consuela exclaimed. There was no one in the corner moments before. She dropped the oven mitts and snatched up a bread knife from the table. Bailey held up his hands in surrender.

"No no!" he said in a loud whisper. "I mean no harm! Uh, por favor. Por favor! The, um, policia coming. Muy policia, grande, muy grande policia..."

Consuela pointed the knife off to the side, sighed and rolled her eyes. "I can speak English, sir," she said wearily.

Bailey lowered his hands. "Well, how was I supposed to know that?" he replied. "Now, listen, you've got to get everyone out of here. Police are coming to raid the house, and they're going to be shooting all over the place. People are going to get hurt. You've got to get everyone out to safety."

Bailey turned as someone walked into the kitchen. "What is going on—you!" Juan recognized Bailey from when he was first brought into the house. Bailey quickly raised his finger to the mouth.

"Wait, wait!" he urged.

Consuela said something in Spanish that Bailey did not catch. Juan replied, and she spoke again. They both looked at Bailey.

"Look, I know how crazy this looks, but General Gomez is coming right now, and—"

"General Gomez!" exclaimed Juan. "He and his men are coming here?"

Bailey nodded his head. "They're on their way right now! Please, you've got to believe me!"

Juan pursed his lips. Consuela could see he was debating what to do next. "I have heard all about this General Gomez from senor Bravo. Very bad man, pretends to be very good man. If what you say is true, senor..." He turned to Consuela. "Gather the other cooks, waiters, groundskeepers, anyone you can find. We must get everyone out." Consuela nodded and started to leave, but Bailey stopped her.

"Everybody except the bad guys," Bailey said. Consuela rolled her eyes again.

"I know what I am doing, senor," she said before dashing out of the kitchen.

"There's two roads coming in here, right?" Bailey said. "I saw it on the map. Gomez will have them covered. Is there another way out?"

"Yes," said Juan. "Through the garden, a footpath through the hills to the west."

"Better get everybody, and make sure that little girl gets to a safe place!"

"Senorita Maria, of course! Senor, I—"

Right then, Benito pushed open the rear door of the kitchen. He was a couple of steps inside, lost in thought, when he looked up and saw Bailey standing by the stove. "There you are!" he spat. Benito rushed forward, swinging his fist wildly. Bailey managed to duck the first punch. He spun around, grabbing a pan off the top of the stove. As Benito turned, Bailey brought it down hard on Benito's head. It made a loud chiming noise. Benito was stunned but not down, so Bailey grabbed the handle with both hands and started pounding on Benito's head as hard as he could. After another strike, the big man was down on the floor.

"I think you got him, senor," Juan said meekly. Bailey was breathing hard. He looked at the pan in his hands.

"I can't believe that actually worked." He looked up, noticing Juan. "Go! Get the girl! We don't have much time before—"

He froze, and cocked his head to one side. Juan started to say something, then he heard the noise as well, distant but getting closer. The sound of a helicopter.

Off to the north, flying low over the hills, Johnson was personally directing his pilot. "Sir, we shouldn't be coming this way," the pilot said. "We didn't log a flight plan."

"Screw the flight plans!" Johnson said. "We need to get to San Cordero before Gomez. Damn that Shamoun! If he wasn't already dead I'd kill him myself!" The helicopter soared dangerously close to some treetops. "Keep it low. I don't want to get picked up on any radar. We need to get in and get out before the shooting starts!"

Unfortunately, sound traveled far over the Columbian hills. General Gomez was checking his automatic pistol when he heard the helicopter, far off, but inconsistent with the normal sounds of the area. "Sir," said the lieutenant, "do you hear that?"

"Yes," Gomez said, holstering his weapon. "I ordered no air support."

"We are nowhere near any airports, sir," the lieutenant said.

"Bravo may have caught wind of us, and is trying to escape. We must not waste time. Are both units in position?"

"Yes, sir," the lieutenant said, nodding his head.

"Let us make our move. All units move in. Give the attack order." The lieutenant went to his Jeep and pulled out a microphone.

"All units: raven, raven, raven!" On the signal, the Columbian troop vehicles rumbled down the west backroads, closing in on the Bravo estate.

At the big house, El Gancho almost danced down the wide steps in front of the San Cordero mansion. He was a happy man. Everything was falling into place. His feet crunched on the gravel as he walked to his expensive car. As soon as Gomez took care of Bravo, his plans—

Gancho froze as he heard the distant sound of gunfire. It was coming from the bunkhouse area. The guards there had not been pulled back to look for the intruder. Only the men at the main gate—Gancho gasped as he saw vehicles approaching from the main gate. They were olive drab in color, and bristling with weapons.

Damn you, Gomez! Gancho thought. I was supposed to be off-site before this! Gancho looked around, at the various guards and gunmen, his fellow Depredators, all looking to him for guidance. For Gancho, the disappointment was overwhelming. He was a man who always played the best hand, always took the most advantageous path. Now, to save face, he was forced to defend the man he had conspired against, and fight the man he had conspired with.

Gancho went to the back of his vehicle and pulled out an AK-47. "What are you waiting for, amigos?" he cried, waving the weapon in the air. "Let's make some widows!"

From his office window, Valentin Bravo looked down on his old friend, El Gancho, and smiled with pride. He could hear the approaching gunfire, and knew his long-time comrade would protect him. He slid a round into the chamber of his .45 automatic and tucked it into his waistband behind his back.

Bravo looked up, and saw Juan in the hallway with his lovely daughter Maria. "Ah, Juan, loyal as ever," he said. "You have read my mind, old friend. Get Maria to the boat and prepare to leave immediately."

Juan, holding Maria's hand, nodded obediently. "I will get the boat ready, Senor Bravo." Juan led the little girl down the wide staircase to the first floor. She frowned when he turned not towards the front entrance but back towards the kitchens.

"Where are we going?" Maria asked.

"It is too dangerous out front, little one," Juan replied. They could hear approaching gunfire. "And the boat will be too dangerous as well."

"What do you mean?" There were several people in the kitchen when they arrived. Some carried small bags, parcels, personal items. Maria spotted the one called Benito, such an awful man, sitting on the floor against the far wall. He seemed to be sleeping. The line of servants went out the kitchen door. Consuela, the head cook was on the stoop when Maria stepped outside. The other gardeners, mechanics and staff were all in a line, hurrying out through the garden.

"You found her!" a voice said. Maria looked around and saw the gringo from the office, the man in the black shirt, standing not far away. For some reason, the gringo looked at his watch.

"Maria, you will follow Consuela now," Juan said, transferring Maria's hand over to the cook. "You must do as she says."

Juan nodded to the gringo, then stepped away from Consuela and Maria. "What are you doing?" Consuela asked.

"I promised Senor Bravo I would prepare the boat," Juan said. "I will obey him one last time." He smiled at Maria. "Goodbye, little one." Before Maria could say anything, Juan was gone.

The sudden sound of a helicopter urged Consuela to move. She scooped up little Maria and followed the last of the staff into the garden. "Papa!" cried Maria. "We left Papa!"

Gomez ducked behind one of the vehicles as a swarm of bullets peppered the doors. "Enough of this!" he cried. "Lieutenant! Fire the incendiaries!"

The lieutenant was prepared. At his signal, three soldiers moved down the line of cars, aimed their weapons, and fired their rockets. Gancho lowered his weapon long enough to see the flaming payloads arc over them and strike the house, exploding on contact, all except one. The last one skidded across the roof and rolled over the far side of the mansion.

The gunmen, surprised by the explosions, took cover after the blasts. Gomez saw his opportunity. "Move in!" he ordered. His men rose and began advancing with waves of automatic weapons fire.

Bailey could hear the explosions as he ran for the truck. Off to the side, he could see the last of the staff filing out through the garden. From his viewpoint, he could not see the little girl among them. I hope she's okay, he thought. Above, he heard something heavy bounce over him.

Something inside Bailey shouted the word INCOMING and he dropped to the ground right as the incendiary mortar exploded. He felt the heat across the back of his neck. He looked up, grass and mud across his face, to see the roof of the gardener's shack in flames. The tree above him rained burning leaves. He climbed to his feet, swatting at the smoke before him.

The truck was parked next to the shack. Bailey noticed new

tires where he had punctured the old ones at the bunkhouse. Flames from the roof and burning leaves were fanning across the tarped cargo. Bailey ran around to the driver's side and flung open the door. He hopped inside, and was grateful the keys were still in the ignition.

Bailey froze. What to do? He had to do something with the container of Shenzhen Wu, but what? The Marines may or may not be on the way, he thought, but he thought of the killers in the junkyard. He couldn't just let them have it. That was when something glittered off to his left. It was sunlight, reflecting off the waters of the lake.

The lake! he decided. He would drive the truck into the lake and dump the canister at the bottom. That would take the whole thing out of the equation. Bailey started up the engine. The gears groaned as he began to turn the truck in a wide circle towards the water right as a man in a white suit appeared at the rear of the house.

Johnson's mind was swimming with demands and obligations. The helicopter he had rented in Medellin swept up dust as it swooped in and landed on the lawn in front of the mansion. The *Depredators* had formed a line behind some cars and were shooting it out with troops from behind their vehicles. Johnson hopped out of the helicopter, blades churning up a wind. He looked at the gunmen, and knew the situation was hopeless. It was only a matter of time before Gomez brought in his heavy weapons.

From the air, he had seen the truck with the canister. It was parked on the far side of the estate, next to the hillside gardens. He had to get to it and make sure the product was safe. The quickest way to the gardens was through the house. Johnson bounded up the wide steps and hurried through the impressive front entrance. Johnson heard thumps up above him as he dashed through the elaborate dining room, then felt the house shake from the explosions. He emerged out the rear of the house right as the truck pulled away from the burning shed

"No!" Johnson cried. He pulled an automatic from his coat. He fired once at the truck as it turned to the left, then held his fire. He couldn't risk hitting the container. The process for making the gas had been destroyed in China along with the lab. All that remained of the Shinzhen Wu was in one singular container. That was his future, his retirement plan—his life, right there on that truck.

He already had shares for sale on the black market, promises of neighborhood-size ethnic cleansing. He had already deposited the money from Gulzar Lajani, to destroy the future of his enemies. Hell, he had already deposited the money from Gulzar Lajani's enemies as well, arranged in secret, so that they could all destroy each other. The world can thank me later, he thought. But none of that would happen if he did not recover that canister.

The first bullet ricocheted off the hood of the truck. Johnson heard the engine roar as the driver floored the gas pedal. Mud and dirt spat up as the truck roared around on the grassy yard. The tarp covering the container caught fire in several places. Johnson stepped away from the house and took careful aim at the driver.

Valentine Bravo saw the helicopter land, and decided that would be a much better way out than the boat. He would have to retrieve his daughter first. Bravo hurried down the big steps and was on the landing when he saw Johnson rush in through the open doors and disappear towards the rear of the house. Bravo looked around, and realized the house was empty. Where was everyone? He hurried down the stairs and stood at the open front door.

The helicopter beckoned off on the wide lawn, rotors still turning, but Bravo could not leave without his daughter. He rushed out onto the porch and crossed where he could see the docks. Bravo felt the explosions, but they were of secondary concern. He was focused on the docks, where he could see Juan preparing the speedboat, but his daughter was nowhere in sight. "Where is she?" he gasped.

The helicopter pilot looked at the gunmen on one side, troops in uniform on the other side, people falling all over and said, "Screw this." The aircraft engines roared, the helicopter rose from the ground, turned, and took off across the lake.

Gancho saw the helocopter land and thought Bravo had called it in. Looking up, he saw it was a surprise to the soldiers, as well. He did a quick count of the troops advancing across the gravel and lowered his weapon. There were too many of them. "Back to the house, amigos!" he cried. The men that still standing ran back towards the now-burning house. Bravo saw them coming and returned to the front door. Gancho stopped at the foot of the grand steps.

"Hold them back, my friend," Bravo said, "I must get my daughter to safety."

Before Gancho could speak, one of Gomez's soldiers rushed forward, his automatic weapon spraying bullets. Gancho turned and calmly fired three rounds into the soldier. He fell, but when Gancho turned back, he saw Bravo staggering, his shirt flooding with blood. Bravo stumbled, dropping his gun, and fell backwards across the wide porch.

Gancho rushed to his side and knelt down beside Bravo. His face was sweaty and pale. "Maria," Bravo gasped. "Make sure Maria is safe."

"Ah, my friend," Gancho said quietly. "I wish I could promise that, but is a violent world, and no one is truly safe. You understand, no?" Bravo stared, and suddenly his face twisted in anger and pain. The old man realized he had been betrayed. His fingers curled and shook as if to claw at the other man. Gancho was not concerned. He knew a mortal wound when he saw one, and he patted the wounded drug lord on the forehead.

With a ragged cough, the life drained out of Valentin Bravo.

Gancho stood, and saw troops in fatigues advancing towards the house. He was about to congratulate them on a job well done when the first couple opened fire. The bullets went wild, but Gancho responded by pumping bullets into the soldiers. They fell, and Gancho retreated into the smoking building. That was when he realized: they were targeting him. He looked back at the body of the solder who shot Bravo. Orders like that could have only come from one man: Gomez.

Johnson fired four times, the bullets crashing through the cab inches over the driver, shattering glass, thumping into the dashboard and shredding upholstery. The truck did not stop. The engine roared as it accelerated forward. Bouncing over garden equipment and flower pots, the truck crashed through the north wall of Bravo's garage, plowing into the building without stopping. Once through the wall, it pushed aside racks of equipment and cans, throwing the interior into chaos. The truck came to rest against one of Bravo's sports cars, a vintage Triumph.

"No, no, no!" cried Johnson as he ran for the ruined garage. Inside, he could see flames spreading. He thought of the warnings from the Chinese scientists. He thought of the millions of dollars that were at stake. He thought of what Gulzar Lajani would do to him when he learned he'd been betrayed. All of that urged Johnson to rush forward towards the wrecked garage.

Inside, the structure was a disaster area. The smell of gasoline was thick in the air, and the flames from the tarp were spreading. Johnson rushed to the cab of the truck. The driver's side door hung open. As he touched the cab he looked over to his left. The driver, the man with the black shirt, stood at a side entrance to the garage. Johnson brought up his automatic.

"It's all yours!" the man cried, and disappeared out the open door. Johnson wanted to pursue, but he had to get the canister to safety. He looked down to see flames around his feet. The truck had plowed through several spare cans of gasoline, and the fire was spreading. Johnson looked up to see large cans lining the far wall of the garage—cans with the lids unscrewed, no doubt by the man in the black shirt.

Johnson cursed as he climbed into the cab of the truck. There was still time to pull it out of the burning building. He sat behind the wheel, his hands slapping against the steering column. Johnson felt a spark of panic. He turned to look around the steering wheel, and the ignition was empty. Johnson cried out in frustration.

"He took the keys—!"

Gomez rose from behind his cover and confidently walked towards the burning mansion. He stopped at the foot of the grand steps to admire his work. Smoke billowed from the upper windows and flames licked across the roof. Gomez turned to the photographer in fatigues behind him. "Are you getting all this?" he asked.

THE SPOOK

The photographer was about to respond when shots rang out. Gomez saw the man fall, groaning, blood spraying everywhere, and he turned to see Gancho standing at the top of the steps, AK-47 in hand.

"Mi amigo," spat Gancho, who leveled the weapon and fired one shot at Gomez. The general spun around once and dropped to the graveled driveway. Gancho was about to gloat when the hand of God struck him from behind.

Bailey could hear gunshots from the other side of the mansion. He could still smell burning gasoline behind him as he ran from the garage. An explosion was eminent. The water would give him some protection—but a year in Afghanistan told him he wouldn't make it. The land sloped downwards, and there was a concrete barrier parallel to the water's edge. Bailey leaped over the barrier and dropped to the ground, hugging close to the concrete.

That was when the rest of the gasoline in the garage ignited. A ball of flame engulfed the entire garage, a wave of heat billowing out as all the gasoline ignited. It lifted the roof of the garage, coughing out from under the gutters, and scorched the back end of the mansion. The grass was on fire. The gardener's shack was on fire. Everything in the gardens lit up in flames.

Bailey's face was pressed against the concrete. He started to wink back home to safety when he thought of the little girl. He hoped she was safe. The others got out, so she must be all right. Then he remembered the *Shenzhen Wu*——the fridge-sized canister on the truck. What was it the CIA lady said? Contents under pressure—

For a split-second, everything inside the garage moved outward at eighteen thousand miles per hour. The heat from the gasoline fire caused the high-pressure canister of *Shinahen Wu* to explode, expanding outward in a burst of energy that destroyed the canister, the truck, Johnson, and the garage, squishing everything within a thirty-foot radius into so many composite atoms. The shock wave first took out the windows on the north side of the mansion, and then it took out the north side of the mansion, blowing off the roof and shoving the burning building two feet off its foundation. Amazingly, the blast extinguished most of the interior flames.

To the troops and gunmen on the south side of the building, it felt like some tremendous weight had dropped on them from the heavens. Fragments of the garage flew a thousand feet into the air and slowly clattered to the ground.

After a long moment of absolute silence, El Gancho opened his eyes. He was lying on his back on Mr. Bravo's precious gravel driveway. Above, the mansion he had coveted as his own leaned over precariously, smoke smoldering from within. Coughing, he rose up on his elbows. All around, the troops and his compadres were prone on the ground, stunned by whatever that blast was.

Gancho knew there was one truth under heaven: he had to get out of there. Off to his side was the cold, prone body of Valentin Bravo. Gancho's eyes wandered to the water, and the docks. Bravo's speedboat was still there, his path to escape and freedom. Groaning, his muscles aching, Gancho rose to his feet, and started lurching towards the water.

THE SPOOK

CHAPTER 26 – LATE SATURDAY AFTERNOON

Tabitha sat in her car, her eyes frantically scanning the papers Bailey had given her. Ideas flooded her mind… but her hands fell limp at her sides. Nothing Bailey gave her could be used as evidence. She could never show the papers to anyone; people would ask: where did they come from? If they were genuine, how did she obtain them? There were serious questions she would be unable to answer. She had to figure out a way to use the information, exploit it, without implicating herself or Bailey, and the clock was ticking. Tabitha buckled her seatbelt, started her car, and pulled out of the cemetery parking lot.

By the time she returned to CIA headquarters and went through the various security checkpoints, she had a plan. "Sir," she said, marching into the conference room. "We have to contact the Columbian government."

"Not now, Tabitha," Weaver said, pointing to the big-screen TV mounted on the wall. "The satellite feed is just coming in." The room was full of a dozen analysists and agents. Hank Gannon sat next to the screen working on his laptop.

The images were of a waterfront estate. The images were grainy and in black & white. Vehicles were formed in a line facing the front of a large structure. "Gomez," Tabitha realized, recognizing the images. "So General Gomez is really raiding the Bravo estate?"

One of the agents pointed to figures moving behind the vehicles. "Looks like they're planning to storm the house," he said. Tabitha faced Weaver and looked him in the eye.

"Sir, we have to stop that raid. It's too dangerous."

"I think the Columbian troops can take care of themselves…"

Tabitha shook her head. "No, no, it's the Shinzhen. It must be there. It was one of Bravo's surrogates that had it sent to Columbia. It was Bravo's men that met the shipment at the airport. He paid for the research. Something that valuable wouldn't be just anywhere. He'd want it close by until he could sell it."

"Mortars," said Gannon calmly. All eyes fixed on the screen, where puffs of smoke detailed at least three launches. Moments later, white bursts exploded across the structure. One exploded behind the house. Smoke started to billow from the building.

"Can we get a better resolution on that?" Weaver asked.

"I'm trying," Gannon replied, bent over his laptop. "The satellite will be out of range soon."

"Sir," Tabitha insisted, "if the Shinzhen is there and a stray bullet punctures the case, it could release the gas on the population. We've got to get the Columbian government to evacuate the area. Hospitals need to be standing by."

"We have structural fires," the technician reported. "Main building and one of the smaller ones on the north side. Looks like the Columbian troops are moving in."

"They don't know how much danger they're in," Tabitha said. "The container of Shenzhen is under pressure and highly vulnerable. If it bursts, the whole country could be sterilized. Who knows how far it could spread before we can cap it?"

"Everything's under control, ma'am," Major Polsky said calmly. "Marine helicopters are already on the way to secure the area."

"Do they have HAZMAT suits?" Tabitha shot back. She pointed to the screen. "Those aren't scientists that have been bouncing the Shenzhen all around the countryside like it was, um, tractor parts. How do we know it's not already leaking?" The major started to say something, closed his mouth, and quickly walked away, pulling out his cellphone.

"We have movement," Gannon reported. The screen showed a vehicle moving out from under the trees. It swerved and crashed into the side of a larger building closer to the water.

Weaver thought for a moment. "Pilsbury," he called. The State Department liaison looked up from his laptop. "Contact the Columbian government. Tell them their forces are closing in on a potentially dangerous biological weapon. They—"

"Smaller building on fire now," Gannon reported. All eyes looked to the screen. White flames were shooting out from all sides. Tabitha spotted a figure running from the building towards the water. She gasped when the image focused for a second, and she could tell the figure was wearing a black shirt. Gannon pointed to the figures at the front of the large building. "The Columbian forces—"

Right then, when all eyes were on the screen, the smaller building burst apart at the center of an expanding shock wave that swept across the satellite image. All the figures on the screen stopped or were knocked flat. The blast seemed to put out the structural fires as well. "What," Weaver said finally, "... what the hell did we just see?"

"Large explosion," Gannon explained in a much too calm voice. "We will lose the satellite feed in sixty seconds."

"The Shenzhen," Tabitha breathed. "The canister must have been compromised..."

"Good God," said Agent Reed, rising to his feet. "Did the western hemisphere just get sterilized?" After a moment of shock, the room swarmed with activity.

"Pilsbury!" Weaver demanded. "Get hold of the Columbian government now! We have a major ecological disaster on our hands. And contact our embassy there, see how many Americans we have in the area." He pointed to a secretary. "Get our staff meteorologists up here—-we need to know wind direction and dispersal patterns. Major Polsky, contact your Marines in the air—!"

"Already on it!" Polsky said, cellphone in hand. As people swarmed around her, Tabitha moved closer to the screen. The image was quickly being obscured with smoke. One figure was moving, headed for the docks. He was climbing on board a speedboat when another figure appeared. It was the one in the black shirt. He hurried down the dock, and reached the far end of the platform as the boat pulled away—and the screen went black. Tabitha turned to the tech.

"We've lost the satellite feed," Gannon explained.

Tabitha swallowed. She stared at the blank screen. That was Bailey. She was sure of it. She remembered the spreadsheet pages he'd given her, and rushed to her cubicle. There were bank accounts that needed checking immediately. There was nothing else she could do. Bailey was on his own.

THE SPOOK

CHAPTER 27 – LATE SATURDAY AFTERNOON

Bailey felt like God had stomped on him. His face was flat against the sandy ground. He'd been through two IED explosions in Afghanistan and waited for the blast to settle. The blast pushed all the oxygen out of the area and it took a moment for his lungs to remember how to start breathing again. He blinked, coughed, and pushed himself up as dime-size fragments of wood and metal started sprinkling down from above.

He rose on his elbows to look around. The big house was still standing, but most of the roof was blown over onto the large lawn. Everything was grey and smoky. None of the soldiers were moving. He looked over his shoulder and saw one person moving, stooped-over and lurching towards the water. From his profile, Bailey realized it was El Gancho. The sound of his feet on wood told Bailey the thug was crossing the dock, headed for the speedboat.

He climbed to his feet, dust and debris falling off him, and turned towards the dock. There was a dusty haze all around him, and he stumbled in a gritty fog. As he reached the wooden planks of the dock, he heard splashing off to his left.

It was Juan, blown off the dock by the blast and floundering in the water. Bailey looked around. Everything else on the dock had been blown off as well, but there was one life preserver left, tied to a post. As he tugged at the life preserver, wrestling it from the post, he heard the speedboat's motor turned over. "Oh, no, you don't!" he spat. He yanked the preserver free from the post, flung it towards Juan, coughed and took off sprinting towards the boat.

El Gancho looked back at the destroyed estate and smiled. He was free. None of Gomez's military would be following him. There were a set of docks across the lake to the north. Despite the smoky haze, there did not seem to be any military activity at all on that side. El Gancho smiled at his clever escape, how he had outsmarted everyone again.

THE SPOOK

Bailey saw the boat move away from the dock. He could wink over, he thought, but he was sure he still had minutes to go before he could flip again. There was no time to double check his watch. The speedboat engine roared as it pulled away from the dock, water splashing high in its wake. He stepped up his pace and aimed for the farthest corner of the dock. Running as fast as he could, he reached the end of the dock and jumped for the boat.

Bailey landed flat on his face on the back end of the boat, hard on his right arm. Pain shot up from the elbow to shoulder. He stretched out his left hand and clawed at the cushions of the boat's rear seats. The impact jolted the craft, sending it off at an angle. El Gancho almost lost hold of the controls. He looked back and was surprised to see his unwanted passenger.

Bailey looked up and saw El Gancho, the gunman's expression fierce. El Gancho took hold of the wheel with both hands and twisted it, turning sharply to the left. Bailey lost his grip. The force of the turn sent him rolling across the back end of the boat to the starboard side, but at the last moment he grabbed the back of the cushions with his right hand. Pain shot up the length of his arm. El Gancho growled with anger. His face snarled like an enraged animal. Furious, he turned away from the wheel and dove at Bailey, eyes ablaze with hatred.

The gunman landed on top of Bailey's back. El Gancho pounded Bailey with his fists. Bailey was sure he was done for...then Bailey remembered that family Gancho murdered in the junkyard.

With a grunt, Bailey gathered his strength and rolled over to face El Gancho, smacking his chin with a backhanded fist. He grabbed Gancho's collar and pulled him closer for a strong left cross. The drug dealer reeled backwards from the punch. The boat lurched, and Gancho fell forwards across the rear end of the boat.

Water sprayed them both. The shoreline zoomed by, and Bailey realized they were going in circles. El Gancho rose up and threw another punch but missed. He shouted something in Spanish. Then he yelled, "Stupid gringo!" as he punched at Bailey's shoulder. "You've ruined everything!"

"Good!" Bailey cried. Grabbing the rear cushions for leverage, Bailey swung his leg up and kicked at El Gancho. El Gancho recoiled from the blow, the hay hook on his belt clanging against the decking. Bailey rose up and saw that the speeding boat had straightened out. It was headed straight back for the docks it started from.

El Gancho followed his gaze. Holding on with one hand, his other fist hammered at Bailey's ribs as the two rolled over each other. Water sprayed across their faces as the boat accelerated towards the dock.

"I could have been on a beach!" El Gancho was yelling. "Instead, we will die together!"

Bailey's eyes focused over El Gancho's shoulder. Beach... It reminded him of ...Hawaii, palm trees, long, sandy beaches, Diamond Head... He remembered the images vividly from a TV show he watched in his youth. He could see it perfectly in his mind.

"I will kill you with my own hands!" El Gancho yelled, raising his fist.

"Sorry," said Bailey, "you won't."

Water sprayed into El Gancho's face, and when he blinked, the gringo was gone! El Gancho's hands groped around, slapping the space where the gringo had been—-right there!

El Gancho looked up. The docks were quickly approaching. No time to get to the wheel, but he could still jump for it. He rose to one knee and prepared to leap, but something held him back, tugging at his waist. He looked, and realized the docking rope was looped around the hayhook on his belt! He looked up just as the nose of the boat struck the eastern docks. "Nooooo...!"

A fisherman far out on the lake saw a large, orange fireball on the western shore. He wondered if it was important.

THE SPOOK

CHAPTER 28 – LATE SATURDAY NIGHT

It was almost midnight on the beaches below Diamond Head. Lights shone from the nearby highway, and there were scattered lights in the hotel windows, but for the most part the beach was deserted. Sean and Diane, a young couple from Shreveport, Louisiana, were up early, walking barefoot along the beach. They were on the island celebrating their first wedding anniversary. It had been a beautiful week. The typhoon that hit Fiji had steered clear of the Hawaiian Islands, leaving clear skies and gentle winds. A cool breeze swept in from the south. The eastern sky was tinged with yellow and orange clouds.

"My God," said Diane, squeezing Sean's hand. "It's so peaceful here."

"I know," Sean said. He breathed in deeply the clean ocean air. "It's like we are the first people on Earth, with the whole world—-"

The scream cut Sean off. It was a long, howling cry, coming in with the morning tide. In the dim light of early dawn, they watched speechlessly as a man suddenly appeared out in the surf, skipping along the top of the water like a stone over a summer pond. Arms and legs spinning like a pinwheel, his howl was cut short when he tumbled into the shallow waters and plowed into the beach's wet sand.

Sean and Diane stood motionless for a moment, astounded. The man suddenly rose on his hands, clothes soaked, covered in wet sand, coughing and spitting. He had on a black shirt and seemed to be wearing fingerless gloves. Sean took a cautious step forward. "Are... are you all right?" he asked as the man slowly rose on shaky legs.

He coughed again, taking a wobbly step. "Oh," he said, "yeah. Sure." He wiped a wet sleeve across his eyes to clear out the sand, but only got more sand in his face. He spat at the sand in his mouth.

"What--?" said Diane, pointing a weak finger out towards

the ocean, "what the hell—?"

"Oh!" said the man, looking down at his wet clothes. He coughed again, and pointed a finger out towards the water. "You, um... you really gotta watch out for that undertow!"

Sean opened his mouth to speak, but before he could say anything the man in black hurried off down the beach, disappearing in the shadows. "The undertow," said Diane quietly, her respect for the ocean suddenly increased. She turned and punched Sean on the arm. "And I wanted to go to Aspen!"

Bailey made it up from the beach, and tried to act casual as he walked down the sidewalk. His clothes were soaked and sand trailed behind him at every step. The streets were mostly empty that time of night, with only the city garbage truck beeping in the distance He made it a block before he stumbled, his vision suddenly blurry.

He stopped to lean against a telephone pole. It was hard to breathe, and he felt very cold. His side ached, and when he looked at his hand it was stained with blood. He felt ill. He started shivering.

I'll be fine, he told himself, but after another block he felt worse. He felt a chill as he leaned on a lamp post. Looking up and down the empty street, he wondered where the nearest hospital was. He needed a doctor. He thought about seeing a doctor...

CHAPTER 29 – SUNDAY MORNING

Bailey opened his eyes. He sat up but felt suddenly woozy, so he closed his eyes and gently laid back down. When he caught his breath, he opened his eyes and looked around.

He found himself on a cot in a simple, Spartan room. There was a small table next to the bed and a folding chair against the wall. The walls were painted cinder blocks, and he could hear someone playing a flute outside. Golden light poured in through an open window. Above him, a bag of fluid hung from a stainless-steel rack. A tube ran to a bandage on his arm. There were fresh bandages across his left side, and his skin smelled like baby wipes.

"Ah, you're awake," Mark said, appearing at the doorway. He put a pitcher of water on the table.

Bailey blinked hard, and ran a hand across his face. "How long have I been here?" he asked, his throat dry with thirst.

"Since before sunrise. One of the townspeople found you wandering in the village and brought you here. You had a low-grade fever. Whatever happened to your side got infected. Your fever's down, at least. We've pumped some antibiotics into you so you should be okay with some rest. Also, apparently somebody beat the crap out of you." Mark examined a clipboard at the foot of the bed and replaced it. "You've been busy."

Bailey nodded. His head relaxed back against the pillow. "It's been a busy week," he sighed. He blinked at the cinder block walls. "This is nicer than the place you were in."

Mark nodded. "This used to be the school. We finally got a new roof up this week."

After a moment, Bailey realized Mark had sat down on the chair and was staring at him. Mark leaned forward, and Bailey could see his black shirt draped on the back of the chair.

The doctor took a breath. Bailey noticed the charitable foundation's logo on Mark's lab coat. He remembered looking up the foundation's website after the lion episode. "I have about a million questions for you," Mark said.

Bailey sniffed. "That's understandable." He could hear birds chirping beyond the open window.

"First off, thank you for saving my life," Mark said. Bailey nodded. "Now, is your name really Jim?"

"It really is," Bailey replied.

"Where did you go after we got to the village?"

"I went home."

"Nobody around here has ever seen you before," Mark said. "No one in the valley or anyone all the way to the coast has ever seen you before. Where's home?"

"Nowhere around here," Bailey said, sitting up in bed. He reached for the pitcher and poured himself a cup of water. It was awkward with the tube in his left arm. He looked up to see Mark frowning. "I'm not trying to be difficult. Really."

"Aren't you?" Mark asked. "You show up out of nowhere and disappear without a trace, then show up a week later beat up with a fever? It doesn't make sense."

"It... complicated," he said finally.

Mark pursed his lips, then stood up. "I'm sure it is. Drink your water. Stay hydrated, and get some rest."

Bailey gulped down the water as Mark started to leave. His Yankees ball cap was stuffed into his back pocket. He stopped at the door and turned around. "Will you even still be here when I come back?"

Bailey started to say something, started to tell him everything, but knew it would take too long, and he had things to do, places to go. His hand holding the empty cup fell weakly to his side. He looked up with eyes meek and grateful. "Thank you for helping me," he said simply.

Mark shook his head. "Whatever," he sighed. He waved over his shoulder and left the room.

Bailey put the empty cup on the table, threw his legs across the bed and sat up. Pulling out the IV needle stung for a moment. He put it in the empty paper cup.

He was still a little dizzy when he reached for his black BDU shirt. His boots were next to the table. As he laced up his boots, he remembered the charity's website. There was an option to make anonymous donations. Bailey made a mental note to do that as soon as he got home.

TIM FRAYSER

He needed a hot meal and a day in bed, but there was one thing he needed to do first before he went home. Something he needed to take care of.

THE SPOOK

CHAPTER 30 – SUNDAY MORNING

"Go home, Tabitha," Weaver was saying. Tabitha blinked and realized she had nodded off at her computer. "You've done all you can here tonight."

Tabitha yawned and stretched. At the next cubicle, she could see the news on a computer screen. "Terrorist threat stopped in Columbia," the headline read.

She stood up, yawning. "Have the CDC found anything?"

Weaver shook his head. "The Columbian government evacuated everyone within a five-mile radius of San Cordero," he said. "Blood tests aren't finding anything unusual. Time will tell, but it looks like the Shinzhen blew itself up before it could sterilize anybody."

"If it ever worked," Agent Conrad said snidely as he walked by. "I mean, there was no test. There's no proof it was ever toxic. We'll never know now."

Tabitha frowned. She imagined Conrad being the guy that gave away movie spoilers on social media.

A tall agent stepped up and handed Weaver a sheet of paper.

Weaver's eyebrows raised in surprise. "Gomez is alive," he said. "They just admitted him to the hospital in Medillin."

"Good," said Pilsbury. "He'll be easy to find when they arrest him for corruption. You were right about investigating Gomez's accounts in Panama, Tabitha," he added. "We found links to bank accounts up and down South America. One had deposits from the Lajani family; Interpol thinks they can link that old buzzard to international terrorism."

"The Swiss government has already frozen the Lajani accounts," Weaver said. "It's funny. This may be the one thing that shuts down Gulzar Lajani once and for all. What made you think for us to look in Panama?"

Tabitha shrugged. "Just a hunch. Gomez hated his cousin in Panama, so it didn't make sense he'd go visit once a month. I figured he must have had other reasons." She did not mention the Panama account numbers she found on the papers Bailey gave her.

Chandra Parks wandered by, a cup of coffee in her hand. "The Columbian police have rounded up the rest of the *Depredators*," she announced. "Most of them already had warrants out for their arrests. It looks like the back's been finally broken on El Gancho's gang."

"Anybody find him?" Weaver asked.

Parks grinned. "They think they found what's left of him in a smashed-up boat," she said. "Good riddance, I say."

Weaver patted Tabitha on the shoulder. "Go home, Tabitha," Weaver repeated. "You did good today. And we won't forget how crucial you were in resolving this situation. I won't forget."

Tabitha smiled. "Thank you, sir. Goodnight—I mean, good morning." She shut down her computer and was pulling her stuff into her purse when Conrad wandered by her cubicle.

"Good job today," he said, hands in pockets.

"Team effort," Tabitha said modestly. Why was he sticking around?

"Whatever came of that black jacket deal from Interpol?" Conrad asked, leaning on the cubicle wall.

"Nothing," said Tabitha. Her eyes felt weary. "When the U.S. military retired the battle dress uniform in 2008, there were warehouses of the things all over the world. They ended up in every army surplus store on the planet. There's thousands of shirts scattered across everywhere. Of course Interpol found pictures of people wearing BDU's. The only amazing thing is that they didn't find more pictures of people wearing BDU's. It was all just a big coincidence."

Conrad nodded silently, and started to walk away. Tabitha stood and looped her purse over her shoulder. She actually thought he'd left when she heard him say, "Where did you go yesterday when you went to get some air?"

She turned to see him two cubicles down, hands still in pockets. "Arlington. It's peaceful there," she said simply. "Helps me think."

"Um hum," Conrad nodded, then turned and left.

Tabitha took the elevator down and went through the security checkpoints. She was halfway home before she remembered: Bailey. What happened to him? Was he alive? She had been so busy with bank accounts and CDC assignments and State Department memos and Marine deployment she hadn't thought about his well-being. She drove home in an anxious state. As soon as she parked in front of her apartment complex, she sent him a text. Are you okay?

She sat in her car and waited. Outside, a dog barked in the distance. Two teenagers laughed as they walked home. A neighbor started up his leaf blower. Minutes passed. Tabitha felt her stomach growl. She stared at her smart phone, but it was silent.

There was no answer.

THE SPOOK

CHAPTER 31 – SUNDAY

Paco trudged along the hot, dry road. It was a long walk from his home to town. It had been a long walk the day before, after reporting the theft of his pickup to the police. The officers he spoke to said they would come back but he never saw them again. It was cold out by the time he returned home. His wife had been completely unsympathetic to his plight, yelling at him for losing the truck.

He missed his pickup. It was old and rusty and did not always run right, but it always got him where he was going. It depressed him to think of the months and years he would be walking to town and back, day after day, trying to scrap together enough money for another truck.

The sun was up and the pavement was already hot when he came to the outskirts of town. There was no traffic on the road, but as he came to a corner a pickup pulled out from the next street up. The vehicle drove slowly towards Paco then pulled over at the curb across from him.

Paco looked close as he walked towards the vehicle. It was a shiny new pickup, American-made, with an extended cab and shiny hubcaps. Just then, a figure climbed out of the vehicle. Paco gasped. It was the gringo—-the man in the black shirt who had stolen his pickup! Paco had been furious, but after a sleepless night he was too exhausted to be angry.

"Habla Engles?" the gringo asked.

"Si, senor," Paco replied suspiciously, stopping thirty feet from the pickup. "I speak English."

The gringo smiled and nodded his head. His clothes were rumpled, and his black shirt was damp and dirty. "Um, I lost your truck," the gringo said. "I know I said I was going to bring it back, but somebody hit it and, well, it's gone. I'm sorry. Um, *lo siempo*. I think I got that right."

Paco frowned at the gringo. He had already accepted that his truck was gone forever. But he did not understand; was the gringo coming to gloat?

THE SPOOK

The gringo put his hand on the shiny hood. "I know it's not your old truck, but I hope it'll do as a replacement."

Paco gasped as he finally understood. "You—you are giving me this beautiful truck?" he asked with a quivering voice. "It is mine?"

The gringo patted the side of the bed. "It used to belong to a drug dealer, a very bad man," he said. "But he won't be missing it. Nobody's going to come looking for it. All the same, you'd better have it registered in your name or whatever you guys do down here as soon as you can. Keep things legal, you know. However those things work. Also, you might paint it. Just in case."

Bailey had seen plenty of activity over at the Bravo estate when he popped up next to the bunkhouse, but nobody was paying attention to the adjacent property. The gunmen had left several vehicles behind unattended. The pickup still had keys in the ignition. A U.S. Marine even waved to him as he drove it away. It only took a few minutes of questioning in town to identify Paco, the old man whose truck was stolen, and where he lived. It was sheer luck to catch him on the way to town.

Paco nodded his head as he ran his fingers over the clean, smooth lines of the truck. He could not believe such good fortune had come his way. "Who are you, senor?" he asked breathlessly. The gringo was pulling something jingling out of his shirt pocket. "Are you an angel?"

"Me?" he asked with a surprised smile. "No, I'm no angel. I'm, well, I guess..." He tossed the keys to Paco in a high arc.

"... I'm a spook."

Paco caught the keys, almost dropping them, but when he looked back, the gringo—the "spook" —had disappeared, leaving the beautiful truck behind.

The gas tank was even full.